TEXTUAL ENCOUNTERS
TWO

Morgan Parker

© May 2013
QuoteStork Media, Inc.

www.TextualEncounters.com

ISBN: 978-0-9917648-8-4

Author's Acknowledgments

This project could not have been possible without the tireless efforts of many people, but I absolutely must thank Leslie Fear, an awesome friend with an even awesomer eye for quality, which will make her a great author herself. Leslie, without you I would not be writing! I owe you!

I must also thank Cathy Givans (CathyGivans.com) who has been with me from the start. She has been my inspiration, my teacher and my friend.

(Added 2014) A huge thank you to Helen Williams for the expertise on the cover design! I could not have asked for a more attractive way to greet my potential readers!

FOLLOW MORGAN PARKER ON FACEBOOK

TEXTUAL ENCOUNTERS - TWO

Located at Broadway and W 26, Toshi's at the Flatiron Hotel happens to pour the meanest martinis in Manhattan. Plus, at just three blocks from my office, it makes for an easy walk after those long days pleasing the Attention-Deficit Neanderthal who calls himself my boss.

In the summer when you can access the rooftop terrace, the view is nothing short of breathtaking. If the architectural view is not quite inspiring enough, then the bankers, lawyers and brokers in their powersuits with their shirts unbuttoned certainly have a way of filling that gap. If I could buy shares in the hotel, I would. Until then, it's a few more weeks before the terrace opens up.

Tonight, Jackie and Romina thought the Flatiron might make for a great night out, just the three of us after a shitty week at work, sipping martinis at Toshi's and seeing what kind of attention we can draw to ourselves.

We walk into the trendy, main-floor restaurant and claim a nice sofa next to a window overlooking W 26. The night quickly evaporates in that magical way that only one drink after another can make happen.

It's dark outside all of a sudden, and there's a pain in my bladder that demands my attention, so I excuse myself. The light-headedness slaps me fast and hard the moment I stand, and it takes all of my concentration to walk a straight line toward the bathroom.

I hear Jackie and Romina chuckling somewhere behind me, but because they have been chuckling like that since 6:30, right after our third round of straight alcohol, I'm not sure if they are laughing at me or something else. Hearing their laughter makes me smile – it has been a fun night so far – and I disappear into the bathroom, lock myself in a stall and try not to fall over as I lower my tights and panties and settle on the toilet to pee.

Beyond that, I remember nothing else. I don't remember the blood, I don't remember rolling forward off the toilet seat and hitting my head on the bathroom floor (yuck) and laying there for God-knows-how-long before a med student found me.

"Did anyone bring you the package that was left for you?" the nurse asks as she jots down notes on a clipboard.

I look around my private hospital room, ignoring the floral arrangements that, I have to say, should have gone to the women who not only knew they were pregnant, but carried their babies to term. The thought makes me want to cry my face off, so I try not to think of it too much.

"No," I manage to choke out. "I didn't get a package."

The nurse nods. She checks the IV tube, throws a band around my bicep and takes my blood pressure.

"How are you feeling today?" She asks.

"Curious. About the package."

She grins. "I think they'll send you home tomorrow. Maybe even tonight." She starts to leave, then looks back at me. "I'll get that package."

She leaves my private hospital room. The silence settles in with the *swoosh* of the door, as thick as a milkshake (fuck, I could go for one of those right about now), and I wonder why Will isn't sitting here with me. Part of me knows the answer, but another part wonders if he might surprise me for once.

Yesterday I woke up to the sound of Will sobbing with his back to me. I pretended that I was still asleep, waiting for him to stop and wipe his face dry. I only opened my eyes once I knew he was sitting up and reading his Kindle. I watched him for an entire chapter before reaching through the bars that keep me from falling out of bed, seizing his hand and bringing it close enough to kiss it.

I don't get to think too much about Will because the nurse comes back and hands me a box large enough to accommodate a pair of toddler's flip flops. The box is wrapped in shipping paper all nice and tight, and has nothing but my name on it, written in black permanent marker. No address, nothing else – just my name in a script that I do not recognize. I stare at the box for a minute or so, then catch myself startled by the *swoosh* of the door again.

It's just the nurse leaving, but I know that any time that door opens, it can bring more flowers and more guests. Maybe even Will. It's that time of day when people will start taking their lunch breaks and, with nothing else but pity on their minds, they will want to visit me.

I open the package carefully enough to preserve the wrapping paper. Ironically, the box has a picture of a popular but inexpensive pair of children's shoes on it, the kind they might hand out at shelters for less fortunate people. But the weight of the box tells me that it holds something more substantial than a pair of cheap shoes. When I remove the lid, I'm instantly confused.

A Samsung Galaxy S4. It's obviously not new – I see fingerprints on the touch screen and the corners show signs of wear – so I'm not quite sure what the purpose of this gift is. I swipe the screen to bring it to life and immediately recognize the photo in the background.

It's Jake.

My stomach tightens. The sight of him makes my palms clammy and my heart rate pick up, something confirmed by the quickening chirps from the EKG monitor.

A whiff of the flowers snaps me back to reality.

I am in a hospital bed.

I am holding a Samsung Galaxy phone.

It doesn't belong to me.

Who sent this? And does this mysterious person know that I just lost Jake's baby?

I scroll through the screens, past the usual and popular apps (games, utilities, anything that hits the Top 10 it seems) and come to the email icon. I click on it, a little surprised to see that the mailbox is empty, or it has been cleared out on purpose by the Galaxy's owner. I wonder why.

My next stop is the jAppe application, a popular texting tool that keeps chats private and secure through some kind of encryption process that leaves the intelligible message existing on only the sender's and receiver's phones.

Surprisingly, I find only one conversation in jAppe.

It is a 3-month conversation between Jake and the phone's original owner, a woman named Katie (who, I am about to find out, is actually *barely* a woman).

With my heart beating a mile a minute, I check my surroundings to make sure I'm still alone, then access the conversation that will change my life forever.

Thursday, April 4, 2013

4:34pm:

Hey, Jake. How's your day been?

Jake

> 4:38pm:
>
> Katie! I'm surprised to hear from you!

> 4:39pm:
>
> Don't you have a paper or something due?

4:43pm:

I figure if I keep waiting for you to contact me, I might be waiting a while. I can't work on a paper when I'm waiting for someone.

4:45pm:

Hope that wasn't too forward of me.

Jake

> 4:47pm:

No, that's fine.

4:49pm:

What's going on at Columbia today?

4:50pm:

I guess this might be even more forward, but I've got nothing going on tomorrow night. Want to hang out?

4:54pm:

Are you ignoring me now?

Jake

4:54pm:

Something tells me it's probably best not to ignore you.

4:55pm:

Something tells me you're right ;-)

4:56pm:

So what do you say? Want to show me what old men do for fun on a Friday night?

Jake

> 4:58pm:
>
> Hey, who said anything about "old men?"

4:59pm:

It's not like I said "geriatric," Jake. Relax :P

4:59pm:

Besides, since I've met you, I have a new appreciation for men over the age of 40.

Jake

> 5:01pm:
>
> Ouch. I haven't fallen over THAT ledge yet. Not even close, in fact.

5:02pm:

So that's a "yes." What time are you picking me up?

Jake

>5:04pm:
>
>Wait a second. How did we get to YES?

5:05pm:

How else will I get to see your driver's license to prove you're not 40 yet?

5:06pm:

That's what I thought.

5:07pm:

Corner of Broadway and W 169. Now you tell me what time?

Jake

>5:10pm:
>
>OK, I guess I can do some babysitting tomorrow night. How does 8pm sound?

5:11pm:

8 sounds good. But the whole "babysitting" comment implies you'll be putting me to bed. Or spanking me. A little creepy coming from an old man.

5:12pm:

Should I bring my pepper spray?

Jake

>5:13pm:
>
>Yes, bring it.

>5:14pm:
>
>I might need it.

>5:15pm:
>
>You scare me, Katie!

5:16pm:

Okay. Pepper spray for the old man and for me, an outfit that makes me look like I'm 16. Perfect.

Jake

>5:20pm:
>
>Great. Looking forward to it.

>5:21pm:
>
>Have a good night, and don't forget to get to bed

early. Old men like me like stay up long after the Disney channel goes off-air on a Friday night.

5:35pm:

Did I take that last one a little too far?

5:45pm:

OK, see you tomorrow at 8pm.

Saturday, April 6, 2013

6:25am:

Are you awake, old man?

6:27am:

Or haven't you taken your shot of nitro yet?

Jake

        6:28am:

        Did you climb out of your crib again? Why are you

        awake so early on a Saturday?

6:29am:

Forget it.

Jake

        6:32am:

        Everything okay?

6:33am:

I had a lot of fun with you last night, Jake. It was the perfect evening. Thank you for that.

Jake

> 6:35am:
>
> I enjoyed it, too. The food was great, the show was decent and, last but not least, you were gorgeous.

6:40am:

Then why didn't you try to kiss me?

Jake

> 6:43am:
>
> I'm sorry. You're a great person, but I'm not looking for a relationship right now.

6:44am:

Who said anything about a relationship?

6:45am:

Jake, I'm a big girl. I think we're both two fairly attractive people, we can be adults about this, right?

6:45am:

Am I wrong?

Jake

> 6:47am:
>
> No, I find you attractive too. And I know you're an adult – remember, the server wouldn't have given you that pina colada if you were under 21.

6:50am:

Then how about you take me to a club tonight to make it up to me?

Jake

> 6:52am:
>
> Things are complicated right now. I need to get my head straight.

6:54am:

Is it that girl you talked about last night? Christina?

Jake

> 6:56am:
>
> Christine.

6:56am:

Yes.

\--

6:58am:

Has she shown up out of nowhere all of a sudden? Because if she hasn't, then I don't see the harm in taking me out tonight.

7:00am:

Unless you have other plans.

\--

Jake

7:01am:

No other plans. Let's do it.

\--

7:02am:

Care to elaborate on "doing it?"

\--

Jake

7:03am:

Very funny.

7:04am:

Let's go out tonight, have a good time.

\---

7:06am:

Will you kiss me?

\---

Jake

> 7:07am:
>
> Possibly. But only if the mood leads us there.

\---

7:08am:

Sounds like you're in trouble. And I'm getting kissed.

7:09am:

Pick me up at 10 tonight?

\---

Jake

> 7:11am:
>
> Sure thing.

> 7:13am:
>
> See you later.

> 7:16am:
>
> You should really come up with a better way to end
>
> a chat. Old men like me don't know when it's

appropriate to put the phone down.

7:20am:

OK. See you later.

7:21am:

Is that better?

Jake

       7:22am:

       Yes. Much.

Turning the phone upside down, I take several deep breaths. The base of my head feels like it's on fire, my cheeks are burning hot with betrayal and I have to clench my eyes shut to get control of myself. I can hardly believe my reaction to this damn Samsung!

Who is *Katie*? I want to kill the bitch. That can be the only way to quell my irrational jealousy, so who is this whore and where can I find her?

Obviously, this phone belonged to *her*. Does that mean she's the one who gave it to me? It would not have come from Jake – not only would I have recognized the handwriting on the box, but he knows me well enough to know how I would react to the kind of texting that was going on between him and this fucking teenager. Shit, he knows something like this would make me wild. And Jake would never do that to me.

The door opens and I snap my attention in its direction. When Will enters with a supportive smile on his face, I secretly curse his arrival while simultaneously sliding the Samsung under the sheets where he will not see it.

"Sweetheart," he says once he gets close enough that I can smell him – a whiff of cologne mixed in with the steady odor that is purely Will. "You're sweating. Are you okay?"

He reaches for the sheets, as if to peel them away to cool me down, but I take a firm grip and keep them pulled high.

"I'm good," I tell him and he gets the hint. He steps back. "I'm sorry," I sigh. "Didn't sleep well last night."

He gives a half grin. "You can catch some more sleep, if you want. I have no trouble just watching you for the rest of my break."

Aaawww, isn't he just the sweetest man on Earth? I smile as pleasantly as I can; not easy considering how much I wish he would just leave so I can get back to the phone. "I think I can stay awake for you." Deep breath – how long are his lunch breaks, anyway? I can't remember. "How's your day been? They tell me I could be going home tonight."

He nods knowingly. "Yes, the doctor mentioned that." He wipes a hand across my sweaty forehead, then frowns. "But I'm still a little worried."

I give him another smile and shake my head gently. "I'm fine. If I weren't, they wouldn't be talking about releasing me."

He puts on his big-boy face and agrees, nodding in that condescending way he sometimes has. And then there's the silence, the unspoken disappointment. Will looks away, and I can tell that he's thinking about something he should not be.

"I'm sorry," I tell him, hoping to distract his thoughts, as if doing so will keep the truth buried. "I didn't know I was pregnant. We've been trying so hard and for so long and... and I should have known." I pour on the tears, not hard considering that I just lost something that up until two months ago seemed like an impossibility.

Will leans in and pulls me into his arms, his firm grip holding me tight. I feel safe and secure with him, always have. He has a solid hold of me and that makes me feel safe. It reminds me why I married him in the first place and for a moment I forget about everything else (yes, even the Samsung Galaxy). It feels like we're the only two kids in this amusement park called life.

* * *

A sound wakes me and I check the clock. It's just after two in the afternoon; I have been sleeping less than an hour. Will has left and taken the flowers with him. With my pending release from the hospital, I nearly forget about the phone, and then set off on a frantic search to find it.

It's exactly where I left it, right under the sheets, and not exactly hidden either. I wonder if Will saw it; he would have known it's not *my* phone, so why wouldn't he have looked at it?

I don't spend too much time trying to figure that one out because I'm relieved it's still there. So I get back to the jAppe application, picking up exactly where I left off.

Sunday April 7, 2013

Jake

> 7:53pm:
>
> Hey, are you still awake or is it past your bedtime?

7:55pm:

If I remember correctly, you were the first one to fall asleep last night. Old man.

7:56pm:

Not used to the stamina of a younger woman, are you?

Jake

> 7:58pm:
>
> LOL. I don't think it's a matter of age.

7:59pm:

Really? You sure you want to have this conversation with a third-year med student? Because something tells me you'll go to bed pouting about it if you do.

8:02pm:

So what's troubling you?

Jake

8:04pm:

> Last night and this morning were good. No, they
> were GREAT. It's been the best weekend I've had
> in a long time.

8:05pm:

Don't get all maple-syrup sappy with me, Jake. We're both adults,
remember?

Jake

> 8:07pm:
>
> Yes. I know. You're right. And that's why I wanted
> to chat.

8:09pm:

I get it. No need to explain. I enjoyed it too, btw. That thing you do
with your fingers on my knee – I start to squirm just thinking about
it!

Jake

> 8:11pm:
>
> I've heard that it has a special effect on women…
> glad you enjoyed it.

8:12pm:

And when you kiss my neck, I swear my knees will just give in and I'll collapse into a mess of physical arousal. If that makes any sense – haha.

8:13pm:

But what I really enjoyed above all of the things you did to me, the things that absolutely pushed me to the edge of self-control, was finally getting a hold of your pants and taking you in my mouth. I've seen my share of men during my rounds and rotations, but I have never craved any of them like I crave you. You're beautiful, Jake. You felt so gentle yet hard and passionate in my mouth, all at the same time.

Jake

> 8:14pm:
>
> We'll have to get together again so I can get a
> better understanding of what you just said. Plus I
> have a lot more that I want to do to you, but I

didn't think you could handle my A-game.

\-

8:16pm:

So it's a date. You tell me when and where, and I'll be there.

\-

Jake

        8:19pm:

        I guess that's part of the reason I wanted to chat,

        too.

\-

8:21pm:

I'm a little confused.

\-

Jake

        8:23pm:

        I already told you things are complicated for me

        right now. I just don't want us to get carried away.

\-

8:25pm:

Of course not. Let's just enjoy each other's company. If we're just fuck-buddies, that's fine with me.

\-

Jake

8:27pm:

No, nothing like that. I care about you. I just can't fall in love with you. I'm sorry.

\-

8:28pm:

LOL. Don't grow a vajayjay on me, Jake. I can't have someone your age falling in love with me – shit, you're almost as old as my dad! Bad enough I have to deal with sad old men at work, don't turn into a geriatric old fuck on me too.

\-

Jake

8:30pm:

OK, point taken.

8:31pm:

I won't fall in love with you. Potty mouth.

\-

8:32pm:

Perfect. Then it's still a date ;)

8:32pm:

Just tell me when and where. I'm free all week after 3pm.

\-

Jake

8:34pm:

Is tomorrow too soon? I was thinking of cooking

for you and then giving my tongue a bit of a

workout somewhere on the inside of your hip?

8:35pm:

Sure, tomorrow's fine. But I can't stay the night. I have a quiz

Tuesday morning.

Jake

8:36pm:

OK, sure. I can drive you home around midnight.

8:37pm:

Good. So we'll meet at your place around 6pm? Gotta run, Jake.

Term paper. GN.

Jake

8:38pm:

Great chatting.

8:39pm:

I'm looking forward to tomorrow. And what I want

to do to you.

8:40pm:

Right, you're gone now, aren't you?

8:41pm:

What does GN mean?

8:43pm:

OH, forget it! Good night.

Tuesday April 9, 2013

Jake

> 5:38am:
>
> Katie, you're absolutely wonderful. I know it was a brief night – I wish I could have kept you until morning – but it was still amazing for me... thank you.
>
> 5:39am:
>
> Let me know when you're done with your classes today. Want to have dinner again?

9:43am:

Sorry, Jake, I have a bunch of schoolwork that I've been neglecting. Maybe this weekend?

Jake

> 10:03am:
>
> I thought you were free every day after 3pm... And yes, for the record? I'm pouting because you're going to put me through withdrawal.

10:04am:

This WEEKEND? That's 3 more sleeps!

10:34am:

Did I offend you?

11:02am:

Not offended, just sitting in class. It's what we students do during the day.

Jake

11:03am:

OK. Text me when you're free. I'll be waiting...

2:16pm:

Maybe dinner isn't such a bad idea, old man. Is that offer still up for grabs?

2:25pm:

Or has Christa magically reappeared in your life?

Jake

2:46pm:

Do I detect the hint of jealousy?

2:48pm:

Because it's ChrisTINE, btw. I think I've mentioned that already.

3:07pm:

Not jealousy. Just wondering when this fairy tale experience with you will come to an end. I know I'm just a placeholder in the big picture of your life, Jake. And that's totally OK with me, I get it. But even riding a crowded subway after a long day is something you'll miss when you have nothing but a walk home in the cold.

Jake

3:12pm:

Holy shit that was poetic. From you? I thought you were the heartless, young princess that is too good for love and feelings and old men like me.

3:13pm:

To be or not to be an old man, that is the question. Besides, just because I'm heartless and younger than you doesn't mean I don't have a brain.

Jake

>3:14pm:
>
>Touché.

>3:15pm:
>
>So you're comparing me to riding the subway? I might have settled for wild stallion, but even then….

3:15pm:

I don't think members of the equine species are still alive once they reach your age. So the subway lasts a little longer, even though the older models get creaky, fragile and smelly.

Jake

>3:18pm:
>
>I'm smelly now?

3:20pm:

I'm talking about the subway. Better get those eyes checked, I think the old stallion needs bifocals.

Jake

>3:28pm:

You're so sweet to me. Maybe I should start
looking a little harder for ChrisTINE?

3:30pm:

Haha, Lance Romance. If you want someone to break your heart
again, don't worry. I know you'll fall in love with me. You'll ache for
me someday. But you can't have me.

Jake

3:30pm:

Sounds like you've taken your confidence pills
today, heartless princess.

3:30pm:

Whatev. Don't ever say I didn't warn you.

3:31pm:

So are you making me dinner tonight or what?

Jake

3:31pm:

We'll see about "aching" for you.

3:32pm:

And just show up at my place at your convenience.

3:35pm:

Perfect, see you around 5:30.

Friday April 12, 2013

Jake

6:47pm:

You were right on Tuesday night. Everything you said was so accurate, I wonder if you're psychic or telepathically read through all of my texts with Christine while I was making dinner. Can you do that?

6:50pm:

Because you were right that I obviously got caught up in something that I never should have got caught up in. And yes, Christine has a scary, violent past. And you also knew that she told me about it once – how did you know that? - so I'm sorry that I lied when I said she didn't. I pretended I didn't know anything about it because it's scary as hell and I don't want you or anyone to get caught up in it. It's her scary past, it's best left there.

7:12pm:

I also agree that everything happens for a reason. I truly believe that. But she and I connected on a level that I have never connected with someone else before.

7:13pm:

So I apologize if it seems that I'm chasing a ghost sometimes. If you ever know the love and connection that I have with Christine, you will understand why it's LINGERING as you put it.

8:15pm:

Jake, let me ask you something. I met you the night you were supposed to meet Christine, right?

Jake

8:16pm:

Yes. She texted me, she set it up.

8:23pm:

Did she ever show up?

Jake

8:24pm:

I think I know where this is headed.

8:25pm:

Even if she had shown up, within a couple of weeks, you and I were screwing each other and you were inviting me out on dates and making me dinner at your place. Now, after this little bit of time together, what if I were to say that you're MY soulmate and I love you more than oxygen, and whatever other vomit-inducing bullshit Christine might have said to you? Would our relationship qualify as the type of love and connection that nobody else would understand? The kind that lingers?

Jake

8:34pm:

No, you don't understand. It was different with Christine.

8:39pm:

LOL x 1,000,000,000! It's not different. There's no such thing as "different." It's just a bunch of words attached to a bunch of moments.

8:40pm:

Don't take this the wrong way. I want to fall in love and be swept off my feet as much as any other woman out there. But Christine was a fraud and the amount of energy and faith you've flushed away with that fraud is a complete waste, Jake. You deserve better than that.

Jake

> 8:42pm:
>
> Are you suggesting that BETTER is you? That YOU are what's better for me?

8:57pm:

I sure fucking hope not. Because I'm just as messed up as any other woman and I can tell you right now that you're not good enough for me.

8:58pm:

But what I DO know is that Christine is not the best person for you. It's time for you to let go of that train wreck and move on.

Jake

> 9:00pm:
>
> You're probably right.

9:03pm:

Want to come over?

11:43pm:

Sorry, Jake. I've gone out with some friends tonight. When you figure your shit out, text me. I'm here when you need someone to talk to.

Jake

11:44pm:

Thanks, Katie. You're an angel. I hope you realize that.

11:45pm:

Damn right I realize it. Now let me get my fun on tonight.

Jake

11:45pm:

OK, go have some fun.

11:48pm:

But not too much fun. I'll be thinking about you and, as you put it the other day, "aching" for you.

When I step off the elevator, the familiar hallway odors tell me that I'm home, as if I spent more than just a couple of nights away. I feel light-headed all of a sudden. I blame it on reading the Samsung while in the car, but just in case it's something else, I kick my pace up a notch and hurry to the door on the left – the door to the Penthouse that Will and I own. I get the keys out, my hands shaking as I unlock the door and make it inside just in time to vomit into one of three vases on the foyer table.

"Are you okay?" Maria asks, coming around the corner. Our pudgy housekeeper/cook looks worried and, when I pull my head out of the vase, I see the same emotion in her eyes that I found in everyone else's: pity. "Let me take care of that," she says, reaching for the vase.

I shake my head and carry the vase back into the hall, heading to the trash room. The last person I want doting on me is Maria. I can bring my own vomit-filled vase to the chute and as I say a quiet goodbye to something Will's mother probably picked out of a discount department store, I feel the Samsung vibrating in my pocket.

The chute door slips out of my grip and slams shut, but I can still hear the vase shatter in the distant garbage bin. The Samsung vibrates again. I stand still inside the chute room and wait. It vibrates a third time.

I feel ill again, my nerves on edge as I reach into my pants and come out with the phone. Tapping the screen, I half-expect a message from Jake. Something intended for Katie, something that will break my heart all over.

Instead, it's a message from Katie, her new phone. I realize I'm holding my breath as I read her three consecutive messages:

\---

Katie2

       4:43pm:

       Hey, are you home yet?

       4:44pm:

       I know you were released from the hospital.

       4:44pm:

       Text back once you're free.

\---

I hammer out a quick response.

4:44pm:

Is this Katie?

I wait less than minute for her response.

Katie2

> 4:45pm:
>
> I'm the one who called the paramedics last Friday at Toshi's.
>
> 4:46pm:
>
> And I'm the one who left this phone for you, in case you haven't figured that out yet.

I'm frozen. I can't move. I stare at the fresh messages on the screen. Like it's something out of a horror movie – something low-budget with a lame-ass title like *Phone Stalker* – and the thought makes me chuckle to myself.

And that's when the trash room's door opens. I almost expect to find Katie there with a knife in her hand and a Grim Reaper mask over her face, but it's nothing that crazy. It's just Maria, looking more worried than ever, too. I can't blame her, considering I'm standing in the trash room (she probably didn't think that I knew where to find it) with a Samsung Galaxy in my hands. I'm sure I look like a lunatic in her eyes.

Frowning, she opens the door a little wider for me to walk through it. "Are you okay?"

The phone vibrates before I can answer Maria. It takes all of my self-control to not glance at the screen. I nod a little too impatiently and we walk back to the Penthouse together.

"Is Will working late tonight?" I ask once we are inside – the foyer table looks awkward without the third vase, but I don't mention that to Maria because it will drive her nuts.

"Yes, he has a dinner meeting with some investors. I expect him home around 8pm."

I nod, the phone vibrating again as Maria and I face off in the foyer.

At last, I give her a nod. "I'll head to bed now. I'm pretty tired from everything that's been going on."

She nods a silent response. Except her nods are quicker and even more awkward than mine. I figure this is a tad uncomfortable for her because she knows about the baby, knows that my pregnancy might have something to do with those late nights and early mornings when I came home and headed straight to the shower to wash Jake off and out of me. Or those other nights when she was out and came home late herself, only to find that the upstairs exit was unlocked because Jake doesn't have a key to lock it when he sneaks out.

"That's a good idea," she admits at last. "Please let me know if you need anything."

I thank her and watch her head back to the kitchen, which is where Maria spends a lot of her time, and then I turn the other way and make a beeline for the bedroom, drawing the phone out of my pocket about halfway there and snapping the screen to life.

Katie2

4:48pm:

I'm sorry about your miscarriage. Physically, you
will start feeling better soon.

4:51pm:

Can we meet for an early lunch tomorrow? We
need to chat.

It strikes me as odd that Katie wants to meet me and have an
infantile chat. But then again, I *am* the other woman, the one who
owns her boyfriends heart and always will.

I start to weigh the possibilities, taking a seat on the edge of the
bed that I share with Will, one of just a handful of places where Jake
has not fucked me with the passion and style that belongs solely to
Jake.

The phone vibrates again and I shudder.

Katie2

> 4:55pm:
>
> Don't ignore me, Rachel. I can tell you've read my messages :-)

> 4:55pm:
>
> I won't bite, I promise. But we MUST sit down and talk. About Jake. It's pretty important.

\-

Now I start to get a little worried. About Jake most of all. I take a deep breath and activate the touch-keyboard and type away.

\-

4:57pm:

OK, Katie, we can meet. Just tell me where and when.

\-

Katie2

> 4:58pm:
>
> When = 11:30am, long after your husband has left for work. So you're safe.

\-

4:59pm:

And what about the WHERE?

Katie2

> 5:01pm:
>
> Where = where it all started.

I don't understand her teenage-quality riddle, something she probably stole from the last Twilight: Breaking Dawn movie, or some other equally shitty film. I refuse to waste time on her games.

5:03pm:

Can you be a little more specific please? I'm medicated, remember.

Katie2

> 5:04pm:
>
> Are you serious?

> 5:06pm:
>
> That night you and Jake went for dinner. The night
> you fucked him?

While I have a hunch about what location she's referring to, the truth is that there have been many dinners, many indiscretions and I honestly don't want to pick the wrong spot.

So I ask her:

5:08pm:
Please, I don't have time for this. My medication is making me sleepy.

Katie2

        5:09pm:

        The night before your wedding. Does that help?

I can't help the tears that start pouring from my eyes. *The night it all started.* Of course.

I tap away at the touch keypad.

5:12pm:
See you there at 11:30 tomorrow.

With that, I place the phone on the night table and bury my face in my pillow, pressing down as hard as I can so I can just let it all go. The sadness, anger and loneliness pours out in wild, choked sobs that leave me gasping for air.

* * *

A little before midnight, I wake up to Will's soft snoring. He likes sleeping with the blinds open and the New York City glow flooding into our room like carnival lights. It may as well be mid-afternoon in Phoenix; I can't sleep like this because I didn't grow up here.

I slide out from underneath the sheets, reach into the bedside table and come out with the Samsung. Heading out into the hall, I feel a little guilty about sneaking away like this, but if I'm meeting Katie in less than thirteen hours, I feel I should know a little more about what she's all about. She scares me a little and the way she speaks to Jake in her texts suggests she might not be the friendliest person in the world.

Plus, if she knows about the baby, then I should beef up my arsenal of knowledge as well, even though I am certain she will always have the upper hand.

Our living room has two leather sofa and four chairs, all of them positioned around a fancy glass table. Although they are "fashion" pieces, the furniture is actually quite comfortable and the view of night-time Manhattan always inspires me. If I want to stay awake, this is the best room for it.

Laying on one of the sofas, I let the coolness of the leather dissolve under my weight. As I get comfortable, I tap the Samsung's screen and pick up where I left off.

Sunday, April 14, 2013

3:30pm:

Sorry for dropping in on you unannounced last night. You can tell I had a little too much to drink.

Jake

> 3:33pm:
>
> No prob. You can tell I had nothing else going on.

3:34pm:

LOL. I'm happy you were home.

Jake

> 3:35pm:
>
> I'm happy you stopped in.
>
> 3:37pm:
>
> How are you feeling now? Still have the headache?

3:37pm:

The headache's gone. I think you fixed that for me before I left ;)

3:42pm:

Still there, Jake?

Jake

        3:45pm:

        We need to talk. You available for a quick phone chat?

3:49pm:

Always.

Jake

        3:49pm:

        Calling.

        8:49pm:

        Sorry about that rambling earlier.

8:50pm:

It's fine. I get it.

Jake

> 8:51pm:
>
> I know the RULES were laid out in plain English. I
> just never thought it would happen. Especially
> with my Christine issues still unresolved. Know
> what I mean?

9:00pm:

Jake, do you remember that second night when you had me over? I
couldn't stay the whole night, so it was a quick dinner and then
straight to the bedroom?

Jake

> 9:01pm:
>
> I believe that was when you compared me to
> riding a smelly subway.

9:02pm:

You actually said I was poetic, Nerd!

9:02pm:

Anyway, I remember lying with you on your bed that night, it was right after that time when you made love to me while holding my ankles over your head. Anyway, we were just lying in your bed after. My chest was pressed up against your side and I hung my numb leg over yours. It was that part where, in movies, the girl lights a cigarette and blows the smoke in your face.

\--

Jake

> 9:03pm:
>
> Of course I remember that night, that exact moment. I remember your hair in my face, it was a bouquet of the sweetest aromas I have ever breathed. You're trying to get me worked up now, aren't you?

\--

9:03pm:

No.

9:04pm:

Well, maybe a little.

\--

Jake

> 9:04pm:
>
> It's working. You have the most perfect toes and that black nail polish you were wearing was pretty hot.

9:05pm:

LOL, I have gecko toes! They're ugly and I didn't know you had a toe fetish. Perv.

9:05pm:

Anyway, I was totally ready to leave and come home once I calmed myself down, but then you slid out from underneath me and at first I wondered wtf are you doing.

Jake

> 9:07pm:
>
> Did you like what happened next?

9:08pm:

Yes! I loved it! When you dragged your finger from my ankle all the way up to the inside of my knee, I had to close my eyes and do everything in my power just to breathe.

\---

Jake

>9:09pm:

>I just wanted to touch you. Your skin is so soft.

\---

9:10pm:

And when your finger crossed over my knee and traced its way up to my ass, that definitely had the impact I was hoping to avoid.

9:12pm:

I wanted you inside me right away, Jake. I had to have you again. There was an urgency to that moment that I have never known until I met you.

\---

Jake

9:14pm:

>When you pulled me on top of you, locked your
>legs around my waist and begged me to kiss you,
>it didn't take long for me to get back into the
>game. I think that's when I realized I was in
>trouble. I was falling for you. Hard.

\---

9:19pm:

I wanted nothing more than companionship from you, but then that night changed things for me too.

9:21pm:

I want you, Jake. Right. Now.

\--

Jake

        9:22pm:

        I want you too.

\--

9:22pm:

There's parking on the street. I'm # 3565C.

\--

Jake

        9:23pm:

        Right now?

\--

9:24pm:

No, ten minutes ago. Get. Here. Now.

\--

Jake

        9:25pm:

        OMW

Monday, April 15, 2013

Jake

> 6:35am:
>
> Your roommates are jerks. Next time you want me over for a booty call, you're coming to my place ;)
>
> 6:37am:
>
> How's the hospital this fine Monday morning?

7:30am:

FYI, my roommates are kind and generous when they're not kept awake all night.

Jake

> 7:32am:
>
> Not my fault you're a little noisy – which I find sexy as hell, btw.

7:34am:

Jackass, I'm not noisy. Plus, it's your fault. Just when I was starting to get used to those fingers of yours, you introduced me to your tongue. You're an evil man, Jake.

Jake

>7:36am:
>
>OK, I'll stop using my tongue if you stop pushing
>me away. Why can't we just agree that we love
>each other?

7:38am:

Nice try. I'm not that desperate to hook up with someone who can't let go of his ex girlfriend.

Jake

>7:39am:
>
>Maybe I can. Maybe I already have let go. And you
>just can't accept that.

7:40am:

Jake, when I can I see you again?

Jake

>7:41am:
>
>When you agree that this is more than just a FWB
>arrangement.

7:41am:

Jake, we can't be more than friends with benefits, not now. And if that means we can't see each other anymore, then I'll have to accept that. It won't be easy, but neither of us is ready for more.

Jake

        7:42am:

        I'm ready.

7:42am:

No, you're not. You can lie to yourself all you want, but you can't lie to me. I'm not ready.

7:42am:

So when can I see you again?

Jake

        7:43am:

        Whenever you want.

7:44am:

So it's a date? Tonight. Dinner and "dessert" at your place. Screaming optional?

Jake

> 7:44am:
>
> Yes. But instead of SCREAMING optional, how about we make it DINNER optional?

7:45am:

Don't make me beg – you know I love a man who can cook.

Jake

> 7:45am:
>
> So you CAN finally acknowledge that you actually love me. That didn't take long! We're an official couple.

7:47am:

Nice try.

Jake

> 7:48am:
>
> OK, dinner and dessert it is. You'll love both, and then you'll fall in love with me as a result.

7:49am:

Aaww, Jake. If I could love you, I would. But love is a feeling I just don't believe in ;)

Jake

> 7:51am:
> That's extremely comforting, Katie. Hurry over after work (MY work, not yours) and we'll see if we can work on that screaming problem of yours.
>
> 7:51am:
> And maybe we'll work on those feelings of yours, too.
>
> 7:59am:
> I'll interpret your silence as acceptance. Have a great Monday.

Tuesday April 16, 2013

Jake

> 12:45pm:
>
> I tried to go for a run, but I just can't get focused.
> Are you sure you can't brush off your class tonight
> and swing by my place instead?

12:52pm:

Jake, every time you send a text, I think of what you did to me the last time we were together. So of course I would love to skip class, but I just can't.

12:53pm:

My parents are going to tear me a new one once they see this term's report card. It's time for me to start doing more of my work and less of you. Sorry.

12:54pm:

It's probably for the best anyway. You need to get your head straight and this is arrangement of ours is obviously messing you up more than we both agreed it should.

Jake

> 12:55pm:
>
> This is messing ME up?

3:31pm:

Jake, you there?

Jake

> 3:37pm:
>
> Sorry for the delay. I'm FUCKED UP, remember?
>
> 3:56pm:
>
> Sorry about that. I didn't mean to upset you.
>
> What's up?

3:57pm:

Jake, I said MESSED up. And besides, you're full of shit. I need to get to my next lecture.

Jake

> 3:58pm:
>
> No, let's chat.

3:59pm:

Maybe later tonight. I don't have time now, the lecture's starting.

Jake

> 4:00pm:
>
> WTF is wrong with you? Why can't I be a little upset with this situation of ours? You come over and make love to me for how many hours? You ask me to come inside you and I'm the bad guy for getting attached?
>
> 4:05pm:
>
> Fine. Ignore me. But I'm not the bad guy here, Christine. You're the bad guy. You're the one fucking with my emotions just so you can get your rocks off. This is NOT right.
>
> 4:11pm:
>
> Forgive me for falling in love with you and expecting that you might actually love me in return.

8:13pm:

Are you still ranting and raving like lunatic old man? Or has the mental Viagra worn off?

\--

Jake

    8:14pm:

    Still at work. I need space. Time to think. Time to

    get my head straight, as you put it.

    8:23pm:

    OK, what's up?

\--

8:24pm:

Jake, go read what you wrote earlier today.

\--

Jake

    8:28pm:

    Okay... What about it?

\--

8:28pm:

Read the text from 405 out loud.

8:30pm:

I

8:30pm:

AM

8:30pm:

NOT

8:31pm:

CHRISTINE!

Jake

        8:31pm:

        Shit, I'm sorry. It was obviously a slip…

8:32pm:

And you wonder why I refuse to get attached to your old pathetic geriatric ass? Jesus, wake the fuck up.

Jake

        8:34pm:

        Katie, I'm so sorry.

        8:45pm:

        I get it. I don't blame you for being pissed off. It's just that only Christine has ever pissed me off that much. So it was a natural response. Definitely not anything personal or intentional. I'm so very sorry.

9:13pm:

I'm sitting here wondering why you're not answering your phone or my texts. I hope you respond soon. I miss you and love you. There, I admitted it: I love you. And this is killing me. But you were right. I'm fucked up. No, I'm more than just fucked up, I'm dying.

9:37pm:

I'll leave you alone for now. Write me when/if you forgive me.

Wednesday April 17, 2013

Jake

> 3:46am:
>
> Katie, I'm sorry about the slip up yesterday. It was obviously not something I said on purpose. I know you realize that.

> 3:47am:
>
> Obviously, I'm falling for you. I'm falling hard. I hate when you do this to me – ignoring me. Give me another chance? I think I might surprise you. You might just end up loving me after all.

> 3:48am:
>
> I can be the man you've always dreamed of. And more. I have no problem working at proving that to you.

> 9:46am:
>
> You know what's weird? I just re-read everything

leading up to when I called you Christine. And you're right. I was a little grumpy yesterday. I was way out of line.

9:52am:
I have a meeting at 10:00am with one of our senior accountants so I thought I would send a quick message to apologize for all of that old man lunacy. It was uncalled for.

9:54am:
What is absolutely TRUE, though, is that I am falling in love with you. And you're right, it's fucking me up in a bad way. I can't stop thinking about you. I look for your face everywhere I go. I close my eyes and imagine the things I want to do to you the next time we're together and when I open them, I feel like I've been dunked underwater. I'm drowning in you, Katie.

9:57am:
When I went back to read our texts, I saw something that bothers me. I'm not ready for you, Katie. I never should have agreed to be with you,

to hang out with you. I was vulnerable after Christine disappeared. I knew it, even back then. But I went ahead and allowed myself to fall for you. I needed time to recover from her. It was unfair of me to drag you into my hell.

9:58am:

So I understand why you're ignoring me. I'll give you a break from my psychosis. And hopefully in a few weeks or months or whatever it takes for me to get my head on straight, you'll agree to meet me again. For coffee. Or lunch. Something safe, so I can look at you with objectivity and determine whether I can be the man you want. And deserve.

9:59am:

I love you, Katie. You've changed me forever. Please remember that.

Friday April 26, 2013

Jake

> 7:32pm:
>
> Hey, are you around?

> 7:34pm:
>
> I wanted to check in, in case you cared. And let you know that I still think of you. Every. Day. I can't escape my thoughts of you.

> 7:35pm:
>
> And I have a confession to make. I went for one hell of a run at lunch today and instead of my usual route, I ran past your apartment. I know it's a little creepy, but I just couldn't remember what you looked like. It's about 2 miles from the office. When I got there, I just stared up at your window and remembered that time we were in your room.

> 7:37pm:

And you were there earlier. I stood there and stared up at you in your bedroom for a good minute to two. I even walked up to the front door. But I couldn't hit the bell.

7:38pm:
I guess the point I'm trying to make is that I CAN walk away. Just like you want me to.

7:40pm:
But I still miss you. Don't think for one minute that I don't.

10:13pm:
Jake? What you just wrote was sweet. Really sweet.

Jake

10:14pm:
Katie, it's so nice to hear from you. What are you up to?

10:14pm:
We're having a party. It's noisy in here. How about that coffee?

Jake

10:14pm:

When were you thinking?

10:15pm:

How about now?

Jake

10:15pm:

You sure?

10:16pm:

Of course I am. But I won't go back to your apartment.

Jake

10:16pm:

Of course not, I understand. You don't want me to be more fucked up than I already am, right?

10:17pm:

It's more about not knowing where I really stand, Jake.

Jake

10:18pm:

Didn't you read my texts? I'm surprised you don't know where you stand, Katie. You're everything to me.

10:21pm:
Still want to meet?

10:30pm:
Sorry, I just stepped out of the shower.

Jake

10:30pm:
Want me to pick you up? Or do you want to meet somewhere?

10:31pm:
Sure, pick me up. But I have a question first.

Jake

10:31pm:
Ask away. I'll answer whatever you throw at me.

10:33pm:
Still there? Or should I just pick you up and you

can ask me in person.

10:35pm:

If it were that simple, I'd ask you in person.

Jake

        10:36pm:

        Oh, a serious question... I love those!

10:37pm:

Well, you probably won't like this one.

Jake

        10:37pm:

        Try me.

10:38pm:

OK. Here goes. If I had unrestricted access to your iPhone, what kinds of messages would I find there?

Jake

        10:38pm:

        Easy. Outside of the work-related emails, all you

        would find would just be messages to you and a

few friends.

10:39pm:

Why, what do you think you'd find?

10:39pm:

I think I would find confessions of love to Christine. I think I would find you begging for some kind of response.

Jake

10:40pm:

Maybe before I met you.

10:41pm:

Jake, I don't think coffee is a good idea tonight.

Jake

10:42pm:

??

10:45pm:

You're lying to me. I know you are. When's the last time you texted her? For real. I'm a big girl, and I want to know the truth.

10:51pm:

That's what I thought.

Jake

> 10:52pm:
>
> Sorry, my battery is dying. The truth? It was
> yesterday. But it was just to see how she was
> doing. I asked if she was ok. I haven't seen her
> since March. Her husband's a lunatic. You would
> be worried too.
>
> 10:53pm:
>
> It's not like that anymore, Katie. I'm completely
> over her.

10:54pm:

Would you have told her that you still love her and would give
anything to kiss her one last time?

Jake

> 11:03pm:
>
> Where is this coming from, Katie? Is it some kind
> of sick joke? You're worrying me over something
> that's buried deep in my past.

11:04pm:

I'm not the one who is full of shit, Jake. You've been lying to me this whole time.

Jake

> 11:04pm:
>
> OK, the truth? You never wanted me to fall in love with you in the first place. Remember? So who cares what I say to someone who has completely disappeared. Who cares if I'm still in love with her. I'm nothing but your fuck-buddy, remember? You made that clear.
>
> 11:05pm:
>
> But that doesn't mean I love her. I don't. I'm worried. Period.
>
> 11:05pm:
>
> All of this would be so much easier in person. If you'd only allow yourself to love me...

11:12pm:

This isn't about love, asshole. It's about honesty. If you can't be honest about the garbage you're texting to other women you claim are buried deep in your past, how am I supposed to trust anything you say?

Jake

> 11:20pm:
> You're right. And I'm sorry. I never meant to hurt or upset you.

> 11:38pm:
> So…. Still up for coffee?

Tuesday April 30, 2013

4:42am:

I know you're awake, Jake. And you know what, maybe I miss you a little too. My heart aches for the sweet things you say and do. But in the next breath, my heart breaks because of all the bullshit you've been feeding me this whole time. You said you can be more than the man I've always dreamed of, but what woman would want someone who shares his heart between two or more women? Why did you have to lie to me? Why did you have to say you're falling in love with me in one breath and tell the exact same crap to Christine in the next when she will probably never get back to you. And even if she does, what about the past two months or so? Don't you see how pathetic you would be for going back to her after she keeps doing these things to you? She keeps disappearing and can't even send you a simple text to let you know what's going on with her. What kind of love is that? It's not love.

4:46am:

Jake, I would like to see you again, but not when you're lying to me.

Jake

> 5:02am:
>
> Katie, I'm sorry I missed your text. I'm still at the gym. Can I swing by your place before work? I want you to see the honesty in my eyes when I tell you exactly how I feel for you. And then you will know that Christine is in my past. When I look into the future, all I see is you.

5:03am:

Sorry Jake. I don't want to see you right now.

Jake

> 5:04am:
>
> ?? Then when?

5:05am:

Once you get your shit together.

Jake

> 5:05am:
>
> What exactly does that mean? Because in one breath you say I can't love you and in the next you tell me to get my shit together. Which is it?

MORGAN PARKER | 85

5:06am:

You can't steal my "in one breath... in the next" saying. Asshole.

Jake

        5:06am:

        I have my shit together, Katie. Please agree to see

        me.

5:07am:

No.

Jake

        5:07am:

        Why not? You JUST said you'd like to see me

        again.

5:08am:

Because you're lying. Your shit's not together. You're still trying to figure out a way to get over Christine so you can win me back.

Jake

        5:09am:

        Okay, so explain to me why it's bad that I want to

make myself available to you 100%

5:11am:
Hello?

5:16am:
OK, how about you text me when you're ready
and all grown-up and we can have that coffee.

3:33pm:
Jake, I decided that I'm going to give you a chance here.

Jake

3:35pm:
You won't regret this.

3:35pm:
Something tells me you're lying again.

Jake

3:36pm:
I promise I won't hurt you.

3:36pm:

That's a big promise. Why not start off small. Like saying you promise you won't lie to me again.

Jake

> 3:37pm:
>
> OK, I promise not to lie to you again. And I also promise I won't hurt you. Ever.

3:38pm:

Only coffee. Nothing else.

Jake

> 3:40pm:
>
> Not even a bite to eat? Like a cookie or sandwich?

3:41pm:

LOL, asshole. I meant no dinner, no dessert. And definitely no sex.

Jake

> 3:42pm:
>
> I wouldn't want it any other way.

> 3:42pm:
>
> The way I see this? It's an opportunity to start off

on the right foot. To make things right. To make you see me as the man I want to be for you, not a fuck-buddy.

3:44pm:

Don't hold your breath.

Jake

3:44pm:

And don't be surprised when you wake up one day and realize that you love me.

3:45pm:

I'll meet you after work. I'll be in the lobby of your building.

Jake

3:46pm:

Good. I'll see you at 5.

3:48pm:

Oh, right. There you go and disappear. Like you always do.

Thursday May 2, 2013

\--

5:43am:

I'm lying here in bed. Thinking about you.

\--

Jake

        5:44am:

        I'm doing the same thing.

        5:45am:

        Was I well-behaved the other night? At coffee?

\--

5:45am:

The ultimate gentleman.

5:45am:

What are you doing tonight? I might just let you take me out for dinner.

\--

Jake

        5:46am:

I would love nothing more.

\-

5:47am:

But it's just dinner.

\-

Jake

> 5:47am:
>
> I get it. Baby steps.
>
> 5:48am:
>
> You're worth the wait, Katie. I wouldn't be holding out like this if you weren't.

\-

5:49am:

Suckit, Jake. Just pick me up at 6 and take me somewhere nice. I'll be wearing a skirt.

\-

Jake

> 5:49am:
>
> You're irresistible in a skirt.
>
> 5:51am:
>
> OK, see you at 6.

\-

Saturday, May 4, 2013

Jake

        2:37pm:

        Katie, are you there?

2:42pm:

Just studying for that quiz I have on Monday. What's up?

Jake

2:42pm:

I want you to know something. I can't think of anything else outside of you. I wake up looking for you. First in my bed – which is weird, because you've only spent the night a couple of times – then on my phone to see if you've sent me a message that's never there, then outside in the faces that I pass as I walk to the subway, and then throughout my day in the numbers I see and conversations that I have. At the office, at lunch, while I'm running in the park, when I leave the dressing room, when I'm walking back to the subway after work and finally when I get home. I'm ALWAYS looking for you.

2:44pm:

And sometimes, when I do see your face in the people I pass, I catch myself holding my breath. I see you in young and old people alike. And you know what I notice, no matter where it is that I see you?

2:45pm:

That hallucinogens are a bad thing?

Jake

>2:46pm:
>
>LOL, no! I notice that you will be beautiful as an older woman. Whether that's in 10 years or 30, you will be a phenomenally beautiful woman, Katie.
>
>2:46pm:
>
>And I want to be there with you to experience it. Every aging moment.
>
>2:52pm:
>
>Are you still there? Did I creep you out?

2:59pm:

I need to study, Jake.

2:59pm:

Sorry, it's all very sweet and kind and everything, but I have to get this stuff done. I'll chat later.

There's a reason I'm reading all of this garbage on the Samsung. And when I hear Will's footsteps creeping up behind me from our bedroom, I realize that this garbage is a secret that I need to keep from him. Forever. So I kill the screen and slip the phone under my thigh where he won't see it.

"Are you okay?" he asks, stopping behind me at the sofa. I feel his hand on my shoulder, massaging the muscles that grow tense at the anticipation of his touch. It's not that I don't love him, it's that we never should have gotten married to begin with.

I remind myself to breathe, to calm down. I let my words out calmly. "I'm fine. Just can't sleep."

"Me neither." He lets go of my shoulder and walks around the sofa to sit next to me. Except when he sits down, he leans forward, his elbows on his knees and his chin in his hands so I can't see his face. He's staring out the windows at the crazy New York City lights. I can see his reflection off the glass and it kills me to find moisture in his eyes, which he thinks he has hidden from me. I've killed this man's spirit. He knows it. He knows everything.

I reach out and rub his back, sending long strokes up and down his spine.

"That was our one shot, Rachel," he says, his voice cracking. "I can't do this again."

"It's all good," I assure him. "Now we know."

He nods, sniffles and wipes his eyes, letting out a tired yet tortured sigh. "I've meant to ask, did Jake ever get a hold of you?"

The mention of Jake's name freezes me and I snap my hand back to my side.

"He said he was at Toshi's that night. He saw them take out you on a stretcher."

"He was there?"

Will gives me a look that says he doesn't believe me. "Yes, he said he was alone. I... I figured he was there to see you."

I didn't notice Jake last Friday, but now I wonder why he was there at all. Did he know something? Was he there to meet someone? Christine? Katie?

"No," I say at last, and even to my own ears the disappointment is crisp and unmasked.

Will stands, wiping his palms down his thighs. I wonder about his nervousness. "Why don't you come back to bed," he says, his voice neutral. But I sense the pain there. "You can finish your texting in the bedroom."

That last part steals my breath and my muscles tighten. He knows about the Samsung?

"I just want you beside me, Rachel. While I sleep." He waits for a beat, the heads back to the bedroom, his shoulders slouched and his head hanging. This man, I remind myself, loves me more than any other living being, even more than Jake ever loved me. Will honored his commitment to marry me and he provides me with a life that exceeds any expectations I might have had with Jake. He never considered calling our wedding off. Not once has Will berated me or made me feel like anything less than his equal. His love, pure and unconditional, exceeds any other love out there. He worships me, he keeps me safe, and he never has to put his feelings into words for me to know that.

But I can't love him in return.

I think we both realize that, so the least I can do for him tonight is lay next to him in our bed. It's not that I owe this to him – I never should have agreed to marry him, *that's* what I owed to him – it's that he deserves it. He deserves more, of course he does, but this is all I can give him.

I get up off the sofa and, catching up to him midway to the bedroom, snuggle into his body and pull his arm around me. Pressing my head against his chest, I breathe in his smell. Will isn't a bad man. He's good-looking enough, too. But he simply isn't my counterpoint.

* * *

The alarm clock reads 4:25. In the morning. At first, I don't know where I am because Will's arm holds me tight against his chest. He's not the hairiest man I know, but compared to Jake's waxed pecks and chiseled abs, Will may as well be a bear. I hate to admit this, but when we have sex, I always enjoy it more when Will wears a t-shirt. Right now, he's not wearing one, so I'm a little grossed out. I know some women like a man with a bit of hair, but I don't. Not at all. I slip out from his grip and roll out of bed, grabbing the Samsung

Galaxy. I sneak out to the living room once again. This time, I'm extra quiet.

My fingers dance across the Samsung's screen, navigating back to the spot where Will interrupted me. It doesn't take long to find, but then I notice the time again – 4:28 by now. Whenever I wake up early in the morning like this, whether it is to run to the bathroom for a quick pee or some other noise dragged me out of my dreams, I think of Jake. When we lived together, he would wake up extremely early to work out. He believed in early mornings and when he returned from the gym it was always around the same time that I would wake up. By the time he finished showering, I would drag him back into bed. Not for sleep.

The way Jake loved me outshone the love that any other man could ever dream of sharing with me. Jake has a magical way with his hands; he can trace my entire body with his fingertips and leave a trail of longing in their wake and a patch of warm, ready moisture between my numbed legs.

I squirm on the sofa just thinking about it. Jake is the love of my life. And even though he broke my heart almost a month ago when he said we couldn't see each other anymore, I know we will be together again. Despite these texts, despite his pathetic fling with this med student whore, Jake will always love me. And that's when I realize something: he wants to see me. It's why he came to the hospital, why he risked everything and spoke with Will in the first place. It's probably why I have this phone in my hands, even though Katie claims to be the one who gave it to me.

As if looking for evidence to confirm all of this, I raise the phone to start reading and notice the reflection in the window. It's Will, but as soon as he sees that I notice him, he turns and heads back into the bedroom. I deliberate going back to bed with him, but opt instead to finish reading.

Monday May 6, 2013

Jake

>6:33pm:
>
>How did your quiz go today?

>6:42pm:
>
>A few months ago, I met Christine's ex in Toronto.
>We had a crazy chat and he told me that the
>woman I thought of as Christine was actually
>someone else. He told me she lied to me about
>her identity and when I confronted her, she
>admitted that it was because she needed to
>escape him.

6:43pm:

The quiz went well. Why are you telling me this, Jake?

Jake

>6:45pm:

You know what's weird? I thought I heard his voice tonight. In the lobby when I came home from work.

6:46pm:

Was it him?

Jake

> 6:46pm:
>
> No, I don't think so. He was just some guy arguing on the phone, and his back was to me. This guy seemed so much smaller than the Peter I remember meeting in Toronto. But the argument was something I would have expected to happen between him and Christine.

6:48pm:

You should have gotten a better look at him, Jake. What if it IS this psychopath? What if he tracked you down because he thinks you know where Christine is?

Jake

> 6:49pm:
>
> Well I don't know where she is. And I don't care.

6:49pm:

I'm in love with you now, Katie. I meant what I
said on Saturday in our texts.

6:50pm:

Jake our timing isn't right. I'm sorry.

6:51pm:

Have you thought about what you'll say if this guy backs you into a
corner?

Jake

6:51pm:

Why are you so interested in this? And he won't
back me into a corner, he's not like that. He's a
wife-beater, which means he's probably afraid of
men. Besides, I am very certain this guy wasn't
Peter.

6:52pm:

I'd be careful. I don't like Christine. She's trouble.

Jake

6:52pm:

Now answer my question about why you're so interested.

6:53pm:

I just don't want you to get hurt, Jake.

Jake

6:54pm:

Because you love me?

6:56pm:

Hello?

7:01pm:

Jake, I'll admit this, but it will be all that you get from me: I care for you. Of course I do. You've been really good to me, plus you're a good cook and you have this special way with your hands. Like when you trace your fingers along the back of my thighs and follow it up with a kiss. Mmmm.

Jake

7:02pm:

I'd be happy to give you another demonstration...

7:03pm:

LOL, I'm sure you would!

Jake

> 7:03pm:
>
> Then agree to see me. Tonight. I want to make love to you, Katie. For you to look into my eyes as I'm about to enter you and see straight into my soul when I tell you that I love you. I want nothing more than that.
>
> 7:07pm:
>
> What do you think? Can I see you tonight?

7:07pm:

I'm sorry, Jake. I'm not ready. Plus, I have to get to the hospital for a 3:00am rotation. I need my beauty sleep.

Jake

> 7:08pm:
>
> Tomorrow, then?

7:09pm:

Jake, I'm not ready. We'll chat on Wednesday. Good night.

Jake

       7:10pm:

       Can I bring you coffee or dinner tomorrow?

       7:14pm:

       I HATE when you do this, Katie. Just leaving like
       this drives me nuts.

7:14pm:

I know.

Jake

       7:14pm:

       Then why do you do it?

       7:24pm:

       That's what I thought.

       7:28pm:

       It doesn't change a thing though. If anything, it
       makes me love you even more. That whole "I want
       what I can't have" factor, you know?

7:29pm:

And yes I realize I'm texting myself right now.

Wednesday May 7, 2013

Jake

        11:45am:

        I was just planning out my run today. Will you be around if I make it all the way out to Columbia?

11:52am:

You'll be sweaty. Gross.

Jake

        11:53am:

        And I'll have to turn and run right back to the office. So it'll be almost like I wasn't there at all. Just how you like it.

11:53am:

Touché.

Jake

        11:54am:

So? I have to get changed... am I running out to you?

11:55am:

Let's hang out for dinner instead. I'm sure that was what you were aiming for anyway. Nerd.

Jake

11:56am:

Nerd? And I'm the old one here? Ha!

11:56am:

I'll pick you up at 6pm. Bring your appetite – I'm taking you to a private restaurant.

11:57am:

I was hoping to dress up like a slut tonight, Jake. You sure you want to eat at some private, swanky restaurant?

Jake

11:58am:

You could NEVER look like a slut, Katie. You're too elegant for that.

11:59am:

We'll see.

Jake

>11:59am:
>
>If I have to dress you myself, I will.

12:00pm:

Damn, you're good. Because now I'll make sure I'm dressed appropriately so you have no reason to put those hands on me.

Jake

>12:00pm:
>
>I was kinda hoping I'd have to make you change...

12:01pm:

Yes, I know. So I'll save you the trouble.

Jake

>12:02pm:
>
>I wish you wouldn't.

12:02pm:

See you at 6, Jake. Enjoy your run.

Jake

>12:03pm:
>
>I'm looking forward to it.

>12:04pm:
>
>Dinner. Not the run. For the record.

>5:15pm:
>
>Are you there?

5:17pm:

Just getting up. You're not cancelling on me, are you?

Jake

>5:17pm:
>
>No. I'm just getting in, even though I left work at
>4.

5:18pm:

Did you walk backwards?

Jake

>5:19pm:

Feisty, huh? Actually, there are cops all over the place. I had to answer some questions about my gym bag (???). Don't know what that's all about...

5:20pm:
Anyway, I'm running a little behind. Could be closer to 6:30 before I get to you. Sorry.

5:21pm:
What did you do, Jake?

Jake

5:22pm:
What do you mean?

5:23pm:
Are you hiding a body in that gym bag? Or does it just smell like a dead body?

Jake

5:23pm:
LOL. Apparently, there WAS a murder. That's why they were asking questions.

5:24pm:

Oh. That sucks. Go get ready, we can talk about it at dinner.

Jake

    5:25pm:

    OK, I'm going to hurry.

    5:25pm:

    See you in a bit.

Thursday May 8, 2013

7:46am:

I saw that murder story on the news this morning. Holy shit!

Jake

>7:52am:
>
>I know, it's super crazy. The police are still all over the place. Not so much here, but I see them at the other building in the morning when I leave and last night when I got home after dinner. I expect they'll be there again tonight.

7:53am:

Are you nervous?

Jake

>7:53am:
>
>Why should I be nervous? I wasn't involved….

7:54am:

Maybe not, but there's a murderer somewhere out there. He seems to like your swanky neighborhood. I'd be worried if it was down here, that's all.

Jake

        7:55am:

        I'm guessing you're not looking to come over tomorrow after your long shift and spend the day in bed with me?

7:56am:

Jake... even if there weren't a murderer out there, do you think it's a good idea for me to spend any time in a bed with you?

Jake

        7:56am:

        Yes.

        7:57am:

        I do.

7:57am:

I don't.

Jake

> 7:58am:
>
> Why not? Explain this to me again. Because last
> night before I dropped you off, there was that
> moment in the car. After I passed my finger along
> your thigh? When you were looking at me? I could
> see it, Katie. It wasn't just friendship. You're
> holding out. I know you are.

7:59am:

I was tired, Jake.

Jake

> 7:59am:
>
> It was more than just tired in your eyes.

8:00am:

LOL, what was it, Dr. Jake?

Jake

> 8:00am:
>
> Hunger.

8:01am:

LOL.

Jake

>8:01am:
>You wanted me, Katie. I know you did. And that pause before you smiled and thanked me for dinner, that confirmed it. Whether you like it or not, I KNOW you. I know who you are and I can see into your soul.

>8:06am:
>You still there?

>8:08am:
>I know you're there, Katie. If I'm wrong... fine. But let's assume that I'm right and you're reading this right now on jAppe. You KNOW that I know you and you're probably sweating a little right now. Or at the very least you're speechless.

>8:09am:
>Because I've hit a nerve. Because I love you so much that I can see through your walls and into

your soul, into who you are. And that scares you.

8:10am:

But that's okay, Katie. You know why? Because you're SAFE with me. I'll catch you if and when you fall. I'll make sure you don't get hurt. Ever.

8:11am:

You're safe to love to me. I won't let you get hurt because I love you too much.

8:32am:

I figure you'll ignore me for a couple of days now. That usually gives you enough time to think things through and send me a text when you're ready.

9:00am:

I know you've seen my last messages, Katie. Most likely, you're deliberating whether to wait those two days, wait and see if I'll contact you first or if you should just jump ahead and reply. I suggest you just reply. Let's put an end to any silence. At my age, you realize that even a minute of silence from the woman you love is a minute you'll never get back, a minute you'll regret letting pass and filling up with something valuable.

9:09am:

I love you and miss you and would love to see you again. Soon.

Monday May 12, 2013

\---

9:27am:

How about that? I went 4 days, Jake.

\---

Jake

> 9:32am:
>
> It was the longest weekend of my life.

\---

9:33am:

LOL, why is that?

\---

Jake

> 9:33am:
>
> I've been checking my phone for your texts. Every.
> Second. Of. Every. Day. You're killing me, Katie.

\---

9:34am:

Sorry. I picked up a 12-hour rotation Saturday that stretched into yesterday. I went to sleep when I got home and am just getting up now.

9:34am:

You know what's weird? Some detectives came by the hospital and asked me about that guy that was murdered across the street from your place. The one we were JUST talking about!!

Jake

> 9:35am:
>
> Why did they want to see you?

> 9:35am:
>
> No offence, but what do you have to do with this?

9:36am:

They said it's because I've been in the area and they tracked me back to the hospital.

9:37am:

They showed me a picture of some guy. Asked if I recognized him.

Jake

> 9:38am:
>
> What did you tell them?

9:38am:

What should I have told them, Jake?

\--

Jake

> 9:38am:
>
> The truth.

\--

9:39am:

Is that Christine's husband? Is that the face I saw?

\--

Jake

> 9:39am:
>
> Wanna grab some breakfast? We can talk about this?

\--

9:40am:

Aren't you working today?

\--

Jake

> 9:40am:
>
> LOL, I called in tired.
>
> 9:40am:
>
> And that wasn't Christine's husband, btw. I met

him last year, remember? He doesn't look like that guy in the photo. Assuming they showed you the same photo they showed me.

9:41am:

The photo was a security pic from the building's lobby. Is that the one you saw?

Jake

> 9:42am:
>
> Yes. You coming over?

9:42am:

You called in tired, and if you're tired, you should sleep.

_____

Jake

> 9:42am:
>
> Can I sleep with you?

9:42am:

LOL, I'm all done sleeping, remember?

Jake

> 9:42am:

Then can I see you?

9:48am:

Hello? Did you ditch me again?

\--

9:53am:

Sorry, just finished in the shower. I'm nervous about swinging by your place, though. With this guy still out there and obviously the police have seen me in the area. That's kind of creepy.

\--

Jake

9:53am:

You're safe. If you were involved in any of this, I'd be the dead guy, not Eduardo.

9:54am:

Better? You want to come over now? I can meet you somewhere so you're not walking alone...

\--

9:55am:

OK, if you'll meet me. What else did you have in mind?

\--

Jake

9:55am:

Of course I'll meet you. And I'll make some eggs and toast. I don't have any bacon.

\-

9:56am:

I'll bring the bacon. I can use it as a weapon if I need to.

\-

Jake

9:56am:

LOL.

9:57am:

It seems a little backwards that you'll bring home the bacon, don't you think?

\-

9:58am:

Very funny. I AM the med student after all.

\-

Jake

9:59am:

But in my version of our future together, I am the one who will take care of you. And you'll only have to work if you want. I'll do everything and anything for you, Katie. Always.

\-

10:01am:

Jake, you slay me. What do you want from me, exactly?

Jake

> 10:01am:
>
> Just. Love. Me.
>
>
> 10:03am:
>
> Are you still coming over after my sappy
>
> confession?

10:04am:

Yes. I'll see you in an hour.

Wednesday May 15, 2013

Jake

> 2:05am:
>
> I just walked in the door. I'm home. Hope you
> sleep well, Katie.

2:05am:

OK, I think I will.

Jake

> 2:06am:
>
> I just wanted to thank you again. These past two
> days have been Heaven for me. But dropping you
> off after the work party was like having my heart
> ripped straight out of my chest. I love you.

2:07am:

Your friend Ben talks a lot.

Jake

2:08am:

He likes you more than he liked Christine.

\---

2:09am:

LOL, he mentioned that a few times! Except he kept calling her Rachel.

\---

Jake

2:09am:

There are rumors that he's officially an alcoholic. I'm sorry about Ben.

\---

2:10am:

LOL, yes, I counted six martinis in forty minutes. Seems harmless enough, though.

\---

Jake

2:10am:

You should meet his wife. Total opposite. But in my line of work, it's about appearances. And my boss's boss is starting to worry that Ben is becoming a liability.

\---

2:11am:

You mentioned Christine... do you know that Ben thinks she's involved in that murder across the street? I think he's serious.

Jake

> 2:12am:
>
> Ha, he probably IS serious. He thinks anything that goes south in my life is Christine's fault. Before her, he blamed Rachel.

2:14am:

Another Rachel? Who is she?

Jake

> 2:15am:
>
> I told you about Rachel. We were engaged and I called it off a week before the wedding.

2:15am:

Oh, right. It's hard to keep all of these women of yours straight. I guess I'm more tired than I want to admit.

2:15am:

I'm going to bed now. Good night, Jake.

Jake

> 2:16am:

> Good night. I'll see you Friday night.

7:35pm:

Hey Jake?

Jake

> 7:43pm:

> You're not working your rotation?

7:44pm:

Quick break.

7:44pm:

I have a question.

Jake

> 7:45pm:

> Ask anything.

7:46pm:

Will you be honest?

Jake

>   7:46pm:
>
>   Yes, of course. I have no secrets from you.

>   7:52pm:
>
>   Still there?

7:53pm:

Sorry, I have a patient I need to see. So I'll ask now and wait for your HONEST answer.

Jake

>   7:53pm:
>
>   OK

7:54pm:

If I were to look through your phone, what kind of conversations would I find between you and these other women? I want names and the status of your relationships with each of them.

Jake

>   7:55pm:
>
>   Are you OK?

7:56pm:

If you ever want to see me again, Jake, you'll answer the fucking question.

Jake

> 7:57pm:
>
> Okay, relax. Can we talk about where this is coming from again? You asked this question already, why are you asking it again? Is it something you saw on my phone? Give me an indication...
>
> 8:12pm:
>
> OK, so you're not going to talk to me until I answer the question?

8:12pm:

No, it has nothing to do with talking or texting. You will NEVER hear from me again, Jake. I swear, if you don't answer me honestly, I'm out of your life forever. And I will know if you're telling the truth, asshole.

Jake

> 8:13pm:

Let's talk about this. In person. I don't know where this is all coming from and I want you to be 100% certain that I'm being truthful with you. Can we meet?

8:20pm:
OK, fine, you're not going to answer your phone when I call. I get it, ignore me. You're pissed. Since you're ignoring me, I will ignore you.

8:32pm:
OK, I can't ignore you. I can't play these games. I'll give you the information you want. All of it. With complete honesty, no secrets. Full disclosure. Will you talk to me once I do that?

\---

8:33pm:
Maybe. Start typing, asshole.

\---

Jake

8:42pm:
Okay, so there's Rachel, my ex-fiancée.

8:48pm:

And Michelle is a girl that used to work with Christine and just recently joined my company.

8:50pm:
And of course there's Christine, who never answers my texts.

9:11pm:
Tell me about Rachel.

Jake

9:12pm:
I already have. We were engaged. I called it off. We're still friends.

9:12pm:
But you're more than friends, aren't you? I thought this was full disclosure, Jake. Did you think I was fucking joking when I said I'd be out of your life forever?

Jake

9:14pm:
No, I know you weren't joking. I will sometimes text Rachel. We get along. It's all good, it's all safe

and that. She's married after all. I get that.

\---

9:16pm:

When's the last time?

\---

Jake

       9:17pm:

       Three weeks ago.

\---

9:17pm:

I thought you loved me three weeks ago, Jake.

\---

Jake

       9:18pm:

       I did and still do, Katie. But you don't love me in return. And that makes me sad. Very sad. Because when I needed someone to help me through some shitty times, like when you ignored me after I called you Christine by accident, I called Rachel. I wish you had answer the call. I wish we could have talked it through because I was in serious pain and all I wanted (and still want, for that matter) is you. To hold you. To love you.

9:19pm:

Or all those other times when you refused to see me. You've left me feeling abandoned and unloved, Katie.

9:19pm:

But Rachel, she was always there for me. Even though she's married, I know she loves me.

9:19pm:

You love her, don't you? And fuck her, too. You motherfucking pig, you still fuck her!?

Jake

9:20pm

Yes I love her – THERE, are you happy? But it's not a romance. It's just sex. And holding. And someone who understands me and my fucked up head.

9:21pm:

Jake, you don't fuck your friends. And you can pay a psychiatrist to understand your fucked up head. Even I can understand your fucked up head, it's not that fucked up. What's wrong with you?

Jake

>9:22pm:
>
>Trust me when I say I DO NOT LOVE Rachel like that. She's a good piece of ass when nothing else is there, when YOU are not there. Because that's all I want, Katie. YOU. But Rachel beats jerking off. She's a warm body when I need it the most. Rachel is my fuck-buddy when I hit rock-bottom.
>
>9:28pm:
>
>You think I'd still be fucking her if she weren't married? If I didn't know her husband takes good care of her? Good enough care that leaving him mean be sacrificing the life and lifestyle she has grown accustomed to? Hell no. I KNOW that I'm just as much a piece of ass for her as she is for me. There is NO love there. None.
>
>9:29pm:
>
>My love is reserved for you, Katie. If you'd only accept it...

9:31pm:

And Michelle?

Jake

> 9:33pm:
>
> Like I said, she's a girl that used to work with
> Christine. I met her at a bar about six months ago,
> maybe less. We text occasionally, have lunch.
> She's married. She joined my company about a
> month ago and she's the most professional and
> honest accountant I know. She's probably going to
> be running the bank someday.

9:34pm:

So she keeps tabs on Christine for you?

Jake

> 9:35pm:
>
> I promised honesty, right? So I'll admit that if
> anyone knows where she is, I figure it could be
> Michelle. So yes we talk about Christine.
>
> 9:35pm:
>
> But even Michelle hasn't heard from her. Christine
> has literally disappeared. Vanished.

9:46pm:

And now for the biggest fish of them all. Christine. Tell me about her. About your textual encounters with this woman you can't let go of.

Jake

> 9:47pm:
>
> Clever, Katie. But there haven't been any. Not since she disappeared.

9:52pm:

I thought we were being honest here, Jake. What kind of shit do you write to her while she's been ignoring your texts and messages?

Jake

> 9:54pm:
>
> Relax, I AM being honest. I'm telling you everything. I send her the occasional text to see if she's around. To see if she's alive.

9:55pm:

And that's the truth? If so, when's the last time you texted her?

Jake

>9:56pm:
>
>What's really going on here, Katie? Why does it feel like my world is falling apart? And like I have no control over it?

9:57pm:

You've made your bed, Jake. Now it's time to sleep in it.

Jake

>9:57pm:
>
>What does that mean? Will you rub my back to help me fall asleep?

9:57pm:

Tell me about Christine, Funny Man.

10:07pm:

That's what I thought.

10:08pm:

Ass. Hole.

The scent of Will's fancy soap wafts over me and I tense up immediately. By now sunlight fills the room and I can't rely on a reflection in the large window overlooking the early city. But I can tell that he's standing behind me, I can hear his breaths and almost feel his body heat. And I can tell that he notices my uneasiness because he steps back, his polished shoes clacking on the floor and his freshly pressed custom suit rippling like paper.

"Are you okay?" he asks.

I don't turn around because the tears in my eyes have no reason to be there. Except to me, they do. They burn from the words I just read about how Jake feels about me. *I DO NOT LOVE Rachel like that. She's a good piece of ass when nothing else is there...*

Will retreats to the kitchen and I wonder if Maria has arrived for the day already. If so, I didn't hear her sneak in.

"Rachel?" Will calls from the kitchen. "You okay?"

At last, I breathe.

"Yes, I'm fine." I wipe my eyes. *She's a warm body when I need it the most. Rachel is my fuck-buddy when I hit rock-bottom.* "Have a nice day."

His footsteps creep back into the living room where I'm sitting. I slip my trembling hands underneath my thighs to hide them from Will.

"Goodbye, Rachel." He kisses the top of my head and lets his lips linger a lot longer than they should for a normal *Have a nice day* kiss. And then there's the matter of his choice of words – Goodbye.

What does that mean? Or in text-speak, WTF?

He touches my shoulder one last time before leaving the Penthouse for his day, which is linked to my iPhone's calendar so I'll know just how late he will be tonight. And if something slipped through the cracks and didn't make the calendar, Maria will know. There's no reason for us to be out of sync.

But I also know that I have an early lunch date this morning. With Katie. The woman that Jake loves. More than he loves me, according to his texts.

* * *

Sitting at the table where I brought Jake for dinner that Friday night so long ago, my stomach sinks at the memory of him sitting him across from me. Even though Will and I have eaten at this restaurant a gazillion times since Jake and I reconnected, it's only Jake that I think about whenever I'm here.

All I think about is Jake.

Still.

Even after he broke my heart by texting those horrible things about me to Katie.

I wonder how I will respond to this younger woman once she shows up. Will I hate her immediately and want to rip her eyes out? Or will I give her a chance to say her piece, to tell me why she wanted to meet to me – although I have a fairly strong suspicion that she will ask me to disappear from Jake's life forever. At this point, I can't say he is worth fighting for, not after what he said about me...

A waitress appears and asks if I would like to order something to drink while waiting for my guest. I ask for a Perrier with lime and she walks off at a leisurely pace. There is nothing hurried about this restaurant at all. That Friday night, right before my wedding to Will,

Jake and I spent hours here after we finished our meal. We chatted, laughed, flirted without the pressure of having to vacate our seats so that someone waiting in line could take them and order the expensive entrees and overpriced cocktails. That night, I felt like the world belonged to us.

By the time the Perrier arrives, Katie is now five minutes late. I reach for the Samsung Galaxy for something to do, a nervous habit of mine whenever I'm stuck waiting for someone else to show up. And although I decided earlier that I wouldn't read anymore of these texts until *after* talking to Katie, I find myself swiping the screen and accessing jAppe anyway. I'm not addicted; I just want to know what else happens between Katie and Jake.

Thursday May 17, 2013

Jake

4:23am:

I'm sorry, Katie. I couldn't stand to deal with this anymore, so I went to bed. My head hurt and I couldn't breathe. My body's reaction to the threat of losing you was devastating. I completely shut down. And this morning, I'm still not fully recovered.

4:24am:

You want to know about Christine, so I'll tell you. I'll tell you everything because I LOVE you. I don't want any secrets between us. I don't expect you to speak with me after this, but if it's the truth you want, it's the truth I'll give you. OK? So here goes...

4:26am:

I already told you about her crazy husband, right?

And you know that Christine and I were supposed to meet the day that I met you. So the worry is always that something has happened to her. Something bad. I keep looking for stories about missing people who match her description and age.

4:28am:

And then across the street, this Eduard Moreno guy gets beaten to death and stuffed in the garbage chute of his building. I know there's probably no relationship, but it was a week or so before this murder that I swore I heard Christine's ex's voice in the lobby of my building. So it's a little messed up, that's all.

4:30am:

After you left the other night, I took another stab at trying to connect with her. I know she's getting my messages and reading them on her iPhone, but for some reason she stood me up that day and still isn't responding. I don't know what it all means so – and this is the part that you will NOT like – I took a different approach than the usual "I'm thinking of you and worrying about you, please write back soon" that I normally send.

4:32am:
This time around, I decided to tell her that I love her and still think of her and that my life has not been the same or even worthwhile without her. I borrowed some sappy shit from that book by Oliver Weaver that I'm reading, and just poured it on.

4:33am:
Something isn't quite right. I can feel it and although I am completely in love with YOU, I'm still worried about Christine. I know that you'll say she left me. I've come to grips with that reality – maybe she didn't want to hurt my feelings with a long and drawn-out break-up, maybe she fell in love with someone else, maybe she just went back to her crazy husband. I've accepted all of the possibilities. But the reality is that I KNOW something's wrong.

4:34am:

I am not in love with her anymore. Every ounce of my heart and mind tell me that Christine is a bad idea. She will ruin me.

4:35am:

But you? Katie, you have a huge capacity to love me. You're independent, smart, funny and beautiful. Just as I know the sun will go down tonight and come up tomorrow morning, I know more than anything else I have ever known that you can love me the way that I want to be loved. To me, you are everything. You are everything that makes me happy. You are my happy.

4:36am:

You will always be everything to me. Get it? I can't breathe without you, Katie. Please write back so I can continue breathing.

3:12pm:

I thought I'd take a shot and write to you. One of the VP's at the office has a summer home in Cape Cod. A few of the senior guys and their wives are heading up for a party and overnight stay this weekend. There's something like 12 bedrooms at this place. If you're up for some time away, I would love for you to come as my guest.

\--

3:33pm:

I'd be lying if I said your explanation of Rachel and Christine didn't make me feel super special.

\--

Jake

> 3:34pm:
>
> It should. Because you ARE special to me. No, you are precious to me. Essential. That's the whole point.

\--

3:34pm:

Jake, I don't deserve you. You're patient. Way more patient than you should be.

\--

Jake

> 3:35pm:
>
> I just want you to love me. And I'll do anything to facilitate that. Patience is easy. I've got lots of it if it means you'll love me someday.

\--

3:36pm:

Jake, you don't want my love. I'm a young woman, stuck in med school for an eternity. You and I are at different stages in our lives. I couldn't possibly give you the things you want.

\--

Jake

>3:36pm:
>
>You already give me everything I want. And more. And once you love me the way I know you can, it will all be absolutely perfect.

\--

3:38pm:

Here's a question.

\--

Jake

>3:39pm:
>
>Ask anything.

\--

3:39pm:

Do you want kids?

\--

Jake

>3:40pm:
>
>Someday. I'm not in a rush.

3:41pm:

What if I don't want any at all, like ever? Or what if I want them yesterday?

Jake

> 3:42pm:
>
> YOU are the worth the compromise, either way. You're worth any compromise.

> 3:47pm:
>
> Are you ok? Still there?

3:48pm:

Jake, you are too kind to me. I'm not special enough for your love.

Jake

> 3:50pm:
>
> LOL, sure you are. So, are you going to come to Cape Cod with me this weekend or what? We can talk about what makes you so special during the long car ride up.

3:51pm:

Let me make some changes to my schedule. I'll let you know later tonight.

\---

Jake

       3:52pm:

       Am I seeing you tonight?

\---

3:53pm:

LOL, not a chance. I need to get my shit together. Clear my head of all things Jake.

\---

Jake

       3:54pm:

       Bad idea, Katie. I'm not a doctor or anything, but you need me in you. In your head that is. That's my professional advice.

\---

3:55pm:

Actually, I'm ALMOST a doctor and I can tell you that you're in my head way too much. Like a headache. I need to get rid of you, at least temporarily so I can get on with my day and life.

\---

Jake

       3:56pm:

I didn't know you fantasized about me so much.

\---

3:57pm:

LOL. Not fantasizing. Just thinking.

\---

Jake

3:58pm:

Anything erotic?

\---

4:01pm:

No, not generally. Not anything I'd admit to you.

\---

Jake

4:01pm:

Then what kind of thoughts are troubling you?

\---

4:02pm:

They're the kinds of thoughts where I try to figure out how I fit into your life and how you fit into mine. Those are the most troubling of all. Because I can't see the solution.

\---

Jake

4:05pm:

Don't let them trouble you. And don't think too

hard about these things. We will work. I'll make sure of it.

4:08pm:

And if Christine shows up again? Looking to get you back? Then what?

Jake

> 4:08pm:
>
> I told you, Christine is the past. She could never just "show up" and get me back. You should know that by now, Katie.

4:09pm:

OK, I need to go. We'll chat later.

Jake

> 4:09pm:
>
> Promise?

4:09pm:

Jake, you're killing me here. Your words... I can FEEL them.

Jake

4:10pm:

Then you know each one was written from my heart.

4:15pm:

Still there?

4:16pm:

OK, don't forget to chat again later tonight.

Friday May 18, 2013

12:48am:

Jake. You awake?

12:55am:

OK, that's probably a good thing. When you wake up, I want you to take two things away from this long-winded text message. The first is that I'm working an 18-hour rotation just so I can spend the weekend with you. The only downside is that I can't leave with you until around noon on Saturday.

12:58am:

The second thing is whatever it is you think you're doing to me... it's working. You've gotten to me, Jake. You're in my head. You're in every breath I take. I just can't stop thinking about you. It's driving me crazy.

1:07am:

I've got to get to work. But know this: you'll be with me for the next eighteen hours. You're in every waking moment of my day and I'm afraid you've infiltrated my dreams too. See you Saturday at noon. It will be a fantastic weekend.

\-

Jake

> 1:32am:
>
> Katie, are you there?
>
> 1:34am:
>
> I'm sorry I missed you. I loved your message, though. My heart's beating so hard right now, I don't know if I should be calling 911. Old guys like me can't take too much abuse when it comes to our hearts. But you're a doctor (or almost), so you know this already. And come to think of it, if I call 911, maybe I'll get to see you this morning. Hmm... something to think about.
>
> 1:38am:
>
> Enjoy your shift and thank you for accommodating me. I think it will be a great time, too. Did I tell you? We will have to share a bed.

\-

3:48am:

Just checking in on a break and noticed your last comment about sharing a bed. Don't know how I feel about that…

Jake

>4:16am:
>
>Then I'll take the floor. As long as you don't mind
>if I poke my head over the edge of the bed and
>just watch you sleep. That's all I need… to be close
>enough to watch you sleep.

4:32am:

Creepy.

4:33am:

But somehow adorable. I'll tolerate that.

Jake

>4:37am:
>
>Yesterday you said that you can feel my words…
>don't you want to feel more than just my words?

4:38am:

Your response doesn't surprise me.

4:39am:

If this is going to be a problem, I can stay home and catch up on the sleep I'm sacrificing... for you.

Jake

> 4:40am:
>
> No, you're coming with me. I'll take the floor. I love the floor, didn't I tell you that already?

4:40am:

I figured that! See you tomorrow!

Jake

> 4:41am:
>
> Enjoy your rotation. And check in on jAppe. I'll write more. Because I love you.

> 4:44am:
>
> It's okay that you don't tell me that you love me too, btw. It's not killing my ego or anything.

> 4:48am:
>
> That's what I thought.

> 2:33pm:

This has been the longest day of my life. Twenty-two more hours before I get to see you. OMG that's a long time...

2:34pm:
OK, so here's a quick run down of who will be there and why you'll care.

2:35pm:
Ben. You met him at the last party. Nice enough guy, but as you know he's a terrible drunk. He'll be there with his wife this time, the one I told you about, who will probably sit out on the deck reading a book and drinking Lemonade all weekend. She doesn't drink because Ben drinks enough for both of them, and then some. Ben still won't remember your name. Just so you know.

2:37pm:
Mitchell. He's the one who owns the cottage. A lot of people find him obnoxious, but it's only because he's richer than everyone else there combined. His wife is his second, so she's a lot younger. Like my age younger, but still, it's

obvious and you need to pretend she's smart. It's not easy sometimes.

2:39pm:

Michelle used to work with Christine. Mitchell scooped her from one of the banks, so chances are good that if you see me with Michelle, she might bring up Christine. She knew we were seeing each other, but that's about it. Her husband is hilarious, he's a property developer or something. I'll make sure he doesn't flirt too much with you. Because I don't trust him.

2:40pm:

Phil and his wife Janice both work with me. Phil was at the last work party, but I don't think you met him. He's an analyst in Oil and Gas and his wife is the admin for Mitch. Great people and they're tight with Mitch and some of the other senior players, so it's important you're nice to them and laugh at their jokes, even if they're not funny.

2:42pm:

OK, that's it. Very exclusive group. Wow, it's not even 3pm yet. Have I told you that I miss you today?

3:47pm:

I'm wiped. I've got eight more hours of this shit. Ugh.

Jake

> 3:49pm:
>
> Maybe it will be easier if I pick you up after work and you can sleep here?

3:53pm:

Nice try.

Jake

> 3:55pm:
>
> Can't blame me for trying, can you?

Saturday May 19, 2013

\-

11:32am:

OK, I'm just getting packing my stuff, I'm pretty much set for the weekend. You can come get me whenever you're ready.

\-

Jake

> 11:33am:
>
> On my way.

> 11:34am:
>
> Are you excited?

\-

11:36am:

I'm wiped. So shut up and just come get me.

\-

Jake

> 11:37am:
>
> Want me to pick up your favorite Starbucks latte?

\-

11:38am:

Now I'm excited.

Jake

      11:38am:

      Perfect. I'll see you in a little bit.

Sunday May 20, 2013

10:58pm:

Text me once you're home, Jake. OK?

Jake

> 11:02pm:
>
> Everything OK?

11:04pm:

You home? I see too many people get hurt while they text and drive. I don't want to hear from you until you're safe.

Jake

> 11:27pm:
>
> OK, happy now? I'm home.

> 11:32pm:
>
> And now you're gone... Everything ok?

11:42pm:

I was just in the shower. You wouldn't believe what took so freakin' long.

Jake

> 11:42pm:
>
> Does it involve touching yourself?

11:44pm:

It might involve a removable showerhead. Read into that what you

want.

Jake

> 11:45pm:
>
> Fuck. My. Life.
>
>
> 11:45pm:
>
> Do you know how difficult it was for me to lay on
> the floor all weekend? Do you know how many
> times I peeked over the edge of that bed and
> found you there, alone on that mattress?

11:46pm:

What would you have done, Mr. Big Talker?

Jake

11:47pm:

I would have started with your legs.

11:47pm:

Started what exactly?

Jake

11:48pm:

Tasting you. Every inch. And from there, I'd move my way up the outside of your body. Kiss my way along your thighs, then your hips, ribs and up your arms all the way to your fingertips. Except I wouldn't have kissed your fingertips, I would have sucked them gently. Each one of them.

11:52pm:

Hmm... I might have enjoyed that. I might have been able to sleep better if I had known someone had just sucked my fingertips clean.

Jake

11:53pm:

OK, now you're mocking me.

11:53pm:

Maybe a little. And you should know that our fingers carry tons of germs.

\-

Jake

> 11:54pm
>
> OK, then, I wouldn't have stopped there. Instead I would have started to work my way back down. Only this time, it would be the inside of your body. Down your forehead, your nose, your lips, your chin and neck. Between your breasts, but that's where I'd take a little detour and trace your nipples with the tip of my tongue.

\-

11:55pm:

Am I still clothed at this point? Because I wore flannel jammies to bed each night and I don't know what that would feel like on your tongue...

\-

Jake

> 11:56pm:
>
> LOL, no. I would have peeled those pj's away so you'd have something dry to sleep in once I finished with you.

\-

11:56pm:

You're suggesting I'd get wet?

Jake

       11:57pm:

       Are you?

11:57pm:

I might head back to the shower if that's what you're asking.

Jake

       11:58pm:

       But I'm not done yet. Because after my tongue has

       traced your nipples to get them taut and

       expectant, I'd move my way down the middle of

       your stomach. Down to that scar, then over to the

       edge of your panties, where I'd trace my way

       along each elastic band.

11:58pm:

I thought I was naked. Dude, you're confusing me.

Jake

       11:58pm:

Well, you're almost naked. No pj's, but still

panties.

11:59pm:

You said something about being wet... does that mean you'll

slobber all over me like a dog? I thought when you said "wet" you

meant, well, down there. Obviously not if I'm still in my panties.

Jake

11:59pm:

Work with me, ok? So now I've taken off your panties and my

tongue is on the inside of your thighs. And you are wet down there,

and not from my slobbering or my tongue.

Monday May 21, 2013

12:01am:

OH, OK, well, let's see…

Jake

       12:01am:

       LOL, are you OK?

12:02am:

Yes, I'll be heading back to the shower.

Jake

       12:03am:

       I have a shower. You can always come over and
       use mine. You know, to keep on your roommates'
       good side….

12:04am:

Nice try. The reason I wanted to write is to thank you for this past
weekend. It was beautiful.

Jake

> 12:05am:
>
> It could have been more beautiful if you had let
> me between the sheets with you.

> 12:08am:
>
> Are you still there? Did I piss you off?

12:08am:

I just need to be sure, Jake. I'm sorry.

12:10am:

But yes, that would have made it even more beautiful.

Jake

> 12:10am:
>
> I wish you'd just let me love you. I won't hurt you.

12:12am:

I know you won't. You're a good man. It's me and my trust issues, nothing to do with you.

12:12am:

And now I need to get to bed. Chat tomorrow?

\-

Jake

>12:12am:
>
>Just when I think we're getting somewhere...

>12:15am:
>
>OK, have a good night. We'll chat tomorrow.

>12:16am:
>
>Hey, I thought you were heading back to the shower?

>12:18am:
>
>So you lied to me... not nice, Katie.

\-

2:15pm:

You're not at work, Jake.

\-

Jake

>2:45pm:
>
>I know. I'm working from home today. Where are you?

\-

2:46pm:

Who's this?

File sent: <img: 21052013_1441.jpg>

2:48pm:

You might want to take note of the file name – date and time.

2:50pm:

And if you look real close, you'll see that it's the lobby of your building where the pic was taken.

2:52pm:

Funny I'm not hearing back from you. She's gone. Are you cleaning up because you're afraid I'm going to come upstairs and deliver this Starbucks to your fucking face?

\--

Jake

      2:55pm:

      We need to sit down and talk about this. It's not what it looks like.

\--

2:56pm:

Who is she?

\--

Jake

> 2:57pm:
>
> Let's talk. I'm on my way down.

2:58pm:

Save your energy, I've already left.

Jake

> 2:58pm:
>
> Come back.

2:59pm:

Her name is Rachel, isn't it?

3:00pm:

She's the warm body when you need it most, your fuck-buddy when you hit rock-bottom. Sound about right?

Jake

> 3:01pm:
>
> You're reading way too much into this.

3:01pm:

What should I be reading into it, then?

Jake

        3:02pm:

        Nothing happened. That's not why she was here.

3:03pm:

OK, I'm coming back.

Jake

        3:03pm:

        Good. Then we can talk about this.

3:04pm:

No. No talking. I want to see if I can smell her on you. Because the way her face is so fucking blotchy, I'm think it wasn't a game of Scrabble you'd just finished playing

----

Jake

        3:04pm:

        You're over-reacting, Katie. Besides, I haven't showered yet today, you don't want to get THAT close to me.

3:05pm:

Oh, stupid me. You're right, I'm over-reacting. And nothing happened. Stupid, stupid me.

Jake

> 3:06pm:
>
> Yes, like this past weekend. How about you get close to me like you did this weekend, except this time I'll get the bed and you can get the floor. Is that close enough for you? Because it's not close enough for me, Katie. You teased me all weekend and now I'm the bad guy.

3:06pm:

Fuck you, Jake.

Jake

> 3:06pm:
>
> Don't do this, Katie. I've offered you everything. Everything. My love. My heart. I shared the deepest parts of my soul to you. You've consumed my thoughts every minute of every day and although I wish I could stop thinking about you, I wish I could just get on with my day and life, I can't. My very existence depends on you. And I

hated it.

3:07pm:

You hate it so much that you're still fucking Rachel and texting Christina.

Jake

> 3:08pm:
>
> In all fairness, it's because of you that I fucked Rachel. And if I can be really honest, you're also the reason I still look for Christine. Not ChristinA – are you dyslexic? ChristinE with an E.

> 3:08pm:
>
> You're EVERYTHING to me, Katie. I need you more than air. But you PUSHED me. And not just this weekend, you always seem to be pushing me away. Why? Tell me why so I can understand why it's such a big deal if I have sex with someone so I don't end groping you and making you hate me? I can't lose you, but I can't go without...

> 3:09pm:
>
> I just want you to let me love you. Like when we

first met. What was so wrong with that?

3:11pm:

For real? What was wrong was that I was the warm body when you need it most, your fuck-buddy.

Jake

> 3:11pm:
>
> But those were YOUR rules! You told me not to fall in love with you and when I did, you completely shut me out. I thought this weekend, you'd see what I'm all about, that I love you and can respect you, even though I'm madly in love with you.

3:12pm:

No, this weekend was all about me knowing.

Jake

> 3:12pm:
>
> Knowing what? Whether you can keep pushing me away? Because emotionally, I'll wait my entire life, but physically if you don't want me, I'll have to fuck someone else. And that's Rachel.

3:12pm:

No, I just wanted to know, to feel, to be certain that you truly LOVE me, Jake.

3:13pm:

Because I was falling in love with you.

3:13pm:

I just wanted to be sure. And that's why I came to see you today. You fucking asshole.

Jake

> 3:14pm:
>
> I seriously can't breathe right now. I can't think. I'm sorry.

> 3:22pm:
>
> I'm sorry. I honestly didn't mean to hurt you. You deserve way better than this. Better than me.

> 6:21pm:
>
> I'd be lying if I said I haven't been in tears over this, Katie. I'm parked outside your house, waiting for you. You WILL have to talk to me.

6:30pm:

I just want you to see my eyes when I tell you how sorry I am. And then you can hit me, kick me, whatever you want. As long as you know I'm sorry and that I love you, I can leave you alone. Forever, if you want.

6:33pm:

Or maybe you can give me one more chance. One more chance to prove to you that I love you and can do this for you.

8:37pm:

Are you okay? You're not home yet. I'm starting to worry about you.

9:02pm:

Don't worry about me. I'll be fine.

Jake

9:03pm:

What does that mean?

9:07pm:

Please Katie, just give me five minutes. I need to see you. I need to explain things.

\--

9:15pm:

No Jake. You. Will. Never. See. Or. Hear. From. Me. Again.

\--

Something distracts me from the Samsung. A sixth sense, like when you look up at just the right moment to stare straight into the eyes of the man you love. But in my case, I'm staring straight into the eyes of my husband. He walks into the restaurant and our eyes meet right away, so I look down to the menu and pretend I didn't see him.

"Shit."

I check the time – Katie is so late now, a good half-hour, that I'm sure she stood me up. I might have considered the fact that she didn't know what I look like, but based on that last string of texts, she not only knows who I am and what I look like, but she has a picture of me from after I slept with Jake. Somewhere on this phone, in fact.

That sixth sense kicks in again and when I looked up, I paste a smile on my face. Because Will's standing at the end of my table.

"Hi," he says. He looks nervous about seeing me here. He takes a deep breath and nods at the empty chair. "You expecting someone? Can I sit?"

He pulls the seat out anyway, sits down and puts his hands on the table. I reach out for one of them, but he draws it back at my touch, reaching into his jacket for his phone instead.

"Sorry," he whispers after reading a quick email. "I don't have long."

"What are you doing here?" I ask him at last.

"I love this place. We've been here a dozen times in the last few months. You know I love it here."

I nod, smiling faintly. "Turkey avocado wrap for lunch. The tomato pesto gnocchi for dinner."

He stares blankly at me for a minute, obviously distracted. Then he shakes his head to snap out of it. He grabs his phone again, but puts it down when the waitress arrives.

"You're here," she says to him, smiling. "Ready to order?"

"I need mine to go," he says. Then to me: "I'm sorry."

He gives his order, I give mine. But he doesn't order the wrap like he normally does. He asks for a salad instead, the quickest one to prepare, and also hands her his credit card so she can create the bill.

Once she leaves, I ask him if everything's okay. "I'm sorry. I wasn't expecting to see you here, wasn't expecting to sit down." Then he realizes something. "So what are you doing here anyway?"

I've been able to mentally rehearse how I would answer that question. "I'm supposed to meet someone. The girl who found me that night." And then I rub my tummy where Jake's baby used to be.

Will gives me his sad and apologetic eyes, just like I was hoping he would. "You talked to her?"

I shake my head, not really expecting the conversation to get this far. "Texted her. She's a little late."

He nods at his phone, his breathing a little hurried, a little nervous for some reason. Must be some huge shit show at the office today, something I'll have to listen to later tonight at dinner, or whenever he drags his workaholic ass home. I'll check in with Maria – maybe something's missing from our synced calendar and I can stop in and see Jake, convince him to cook me something nice. Sounds like he was looking for me anyway.

"You should text her," Will says. His voice tells me something horrible is going on. Some days, he hates his job. "You know, to make sure she's still showing up. I'll be gone, in case she gets here and sees you with someone."

I grab the Samsung absently. "Oh, right. Sure."

I tap away with Will's eyes on me.

\---

10:15am:

Me: Are we still meeting? Or have you stood me up?

\---

I press Send. Coincidentally, Will's phone vibrates on the table — *bzzt, bzzt* — but he doesn't seem to notice. He's staring straight at me. No, not *at* me, but *through* me.

"Everything okay, Will?" I ask, nodding at his phone. "You going to get that?"

He shakes his head. He's so distracted I'm sincerely worried about the mess he's dealing with at the office right now. How *bad* is it?

"You're not yourself," I tell him, then smile.

The waitress returns, providing him with a legitimate excuse to delay answering me. She hands him the credit card and bill, then tells him his take-out salad is at the bar. "Whenever you're ready." And then she walks away, and Will watches her all the way back to the bar where there's a plastic white bag with a large salad in it.

"Has Katie gotten back to you?" he asks, grabbing his phone. But he's so distracted and I'm so worried about him that I don't even pick up on the fact that he knows her name. He stands up. "I'm going to get my salad."

I grab the phone and see if she responded. No. She hasn't even read the message on jAppe – but then the D for Delivered changes to an R for Read. I glance at Will, who's tapping away en route to the bar.

The Samsung vibrates. I pick it up and see Katie's response.

10:18am:

Katie2: I'm here.

I look around, trying to find a young woman, the young whore who almost managed to convince Jake that he loved her enough to give me up. But there are no other singles at the restaurant. In fact, there are no other women my age or younger. All older, all in business suits.

I tap away at the screen.

10:19am:

Me: Where are you? I don't see you???

I wait less than a minute for a response, but it was long enough to keep me at the edge of my seat. Where is she?

10:19am:

Katie2: I'm at the bar.

Except when I look at the bar, there is only one person there: Will. With his back to me, he just stands there like he's waiting for something. I don't know what that could be, though. His salad is ready and there are no servers behind the bar.

And then I notice his shoulders, their jerking motion. He's crying. Oh my, he's crying to himself, alone at the bar. I feel sorry for him until the realization sinks in.

At the nearest table, our waitress is distracted by Will's quiet sobs and she stops writing orders long enough to look at him. Her face drops. It tells me something's wrong. As if sensing my eyes on her, she glances my way, but quickly turns her attention back to the patrons at her table.

Fuck. Me.

I tap four quick words into the Samsung and wait.

10:20am:

Me: Will, is that you?

10:20am:

You need to move out. Be gone before I get home tonight.

With that, his shoulders calm. I watch Will from behind as he pockets his phone and straightens his back, and without so much as looking at me one last time, he grabs his salad and walks away from the bar.

After he leaves through the restaurant's doors, I feel a shiver run through me. That sixth sense kicks in again and I catch the waitress watching me, her eyes reflecting the shock on my own face.

And then the Samsung vibrates again. I snatch it up.

10:21pm:

Katie2: You're a fucking whore.

----

* * *

It's the longest wait for a cab I have ever experienced and it feels like everyone is looking at me, blaming me with their hateful and accusing eyes. It's my fault for everything. Eventually a taxi pulls to a stop and just as I settle into the back seat it starts raining. Actually it starts pouring.

"Where to, lady." Even the cab driver sounds accusatory.

And because I don't know where I'm going or where I should go, his tone becomes even *more* accusatory.

"Lady, I don't have all freaking day. Where to?"

Funny, it seems we're already moving and the meter is already running; the longer I'm here, the more he gets paid. But since he wants a smaller fare, I rhyme off the Penthouse address. I'll have to pack a few things; I'll let the divorce attorney's office get the rest of my stuff whenever the ink dries. The driver knows my address according to the nod he gives me and we speed up to a slightly quicker crawl.

While wading through traffic, I wonder how everything turned south so quickly. How come I assumed it was Katie who found me in the bathroom at Toshi's. Or at least why did I think it was Katie who wanted to meet me at the restaurant today.

I rest my head back against the seat. It doesn't matter. None of it matters. Will is right to hate me, I never loved him in the first place, and right now I just broke his heart. He's a good man, he never deserved any of this. Fuck, what have I done?

I reach down and retrieve the Samsung. There's still a little left to read. I swipe at the screen and return to jAppe with a feeling in my stomach like my life is now over.

Monday June 24, 2013

Jake

2:36pm:

Katie, it's been over a month. Can you please give me the time of day?

2:57pm:

I was speaking with Mitchell this morning and he asked about you. That's probably why I'm writing to you now. The way he looked at me when I said we haven't spoken since shortly after his weekend party only enhanced the pain I've been feeling since you saw what you think you saw.

3:00pm:

For the record, I have asked Rachel to never contact me again. We're through. Forever. I never told you how she almost ruined my relationship with Christine by showing up in my life and fucking with my head. She's married. She needs to spend her time with her husband. Not me. She had her

chance with me, but she blew it. I can't keep
playing those games with her.

\---

3:03pm:

She's a whore, Jake. Fucking you while fucking her husband. A
cheating whore. And to be fair, you're equally to blame. You told
me you loved me. Now I want nothing to do with you.

\---

Jake

> 3:04pm:
>
> You're right. I hate Rachel for this.

\---

3:04pm:

Funny. I hate YOU for this.

\---

Jake

> 3:05pm:
>
> I don't hate her because of her addiction to sex –
> who knows how many other guys she is fucking
> behind my back – but because this is fucking up
> my relationship with you. I love you, Katie. I know
> that more than I've known anything else in my life.
> I. Love. You.

\---

3:05pm:

That's where you're wrong. SHE isn't the reason you'll never have another chance at me. YOU are the reason for that. And she's no more addicted to sex than you are. You two are perfect for each other and I wish you both nothing but the worst.

\---

Jake

> 3:06pm:
>
> Fair enough. It takes two, right? I could have- no, I SHOULD have pushed her away when I had the chance. I didn't. And although I'm not blaming you, remember this: YOU kept pushing ME away. You knew how I feel yet you kept pushing? We had all weekend together, what else was I supposed to think?

\---

3:08pm:

I DID love you, Jake. From that very first day, my heart was yours. And now that it's broken and bleeding, I blame you.

\---

Jake

> 3:09pm:
>
> You sure had a strange way of showing me that you love me. The whole "let's be fuck-buddies"

followed by "let's be friends" in the last few
weeks. WTF was I supposed to think? That you
love me? Not a chance. I felt like I was constantly
fighting for you attention, for you to open up. All I
wanted was your love.

3:11pm:

Love is my weakness, Jake. I didn't want you to see mine.

Jake

3:12pm:

No, you're wrong about that.

3:14pm:

Love makes you smart and strong. Smart enough
to know there is nothing else that matters. Strong
enough to know that nothing else can weaken
you. When you're in love, you're at peace, you're
whole and you're always safe. I KNOW I made you
feel at peace. And I KNOW I always made you feel
safe.

3:14pm:

And while I can't speak for you, I ALWAYS felt

whole whenever we were together. Even when we weren't together, just knowing you were there and I'd get another chance at loving you, I felt I had found my counterpoint. I've said that before, I know I have.

3:16pm:

Yes, you have. I don't know what it means, but you've said it before.

Jake

>3:16pm:
>
>It's a technical term I heard on the classical music station. I know that sounds cold and un-romantic, but it fits. It's where you have two very different musical melodies that, individually, play extremely beautifully. But when you put them together, they're harmonious. When I heard it, I thought of us. I have my life, you have yours. When we are together, my life is even more harmonious.

>3:18pm:
>
>Or at least it was more harmonious for me. Whenever we were together, my world was beautiful. It makes me sad that you don't know

what I'm talking about. Maybe we are better off as friends...?

3:19pm:

No, not friends. Not anything. Because I can't do this. I can't go from opening myself up one second to shutting myself down entirely the next. Seeing that whore leave your building with rosy, post-orgasm cheeks and a smug grin on her face made me realize something. It's better to say goodbye to you. Because you are a beaten wife, Jake. You'll always go back to her. And I can't love a beaten wife.

Jake

3:21pm:

You're right, she abused me long enough. But it has ended. You've given me the strength I need to get over her. Because like I said earlier love makes you strong and smart. She had a chance to fight for me. She didn't. All she did was show up before her wedding day. I was pathetic. When she said she was getting married that morning, I begged her to stay.

3:35pm:

Goodbye, Jake.

Jake

3:36pm:

No, not goodbye. I will continue to FIGHT for you,
Katie. Like I'm always fighting for you because I
know that begging didn't work for Rachel and it
sure won't work for you.

3:37pm:

You see, I begged her to stick around to see how I
was the better choice. Begged her to let me show
her how I could make her happier than the man
she chose instead of me, the man she married. I
could have made her happier than ANY man.

3:40pm:

So you know how it feels. When the person you love picks someone
else.

Jake

3:41pm:

Yes. I do. It's why I gave you so much time this
past month.

3:44pm:

And you're forgetting something. I didn't pick Rachel over of you. I might have slept with her, but that's not love. It was just sex. That's it.

3:45pm:

Something I never told ANYONE was when we had sex that Friday night, the next morning when she was gone, I lost it. I cried and cried – it was the worst feeling I have ever had, to feel completely abandoned and lost without someone else. She came back, though. I still don't know why, but I suspect it was to say goodbye while still keeping that door open for our friendly encounters. I really thought we could make things work. I told her we could pick up exactly where we left off. She disagreed. I begged her to not marry this guy. Raw emotion was pouring out of my mouth, my eyes, I felt like I was sacrificing my soul out to her. I guess I was. And all she did was sit on the edge of the bed while I was on the floor, latched on to her ankles, begging at her feet. I was like a dog, Katie. A fucking dog. You know what she did?

3:47pm:

She had "just sex" with you?

Jake

>3:47pm:
>
>Very funny. I'm pouring my heart out to you and you decided to be funny. Good one.

>3:48pm:
>
>Actually, what she did was stand up and step out of my grip. She walked over me like I was a piece of trash, and as she left she told me: You had your chance, it's over.

3:48pm:

So this isn't new for you.

Jake

>3:50pm:
>
>That hurt. A lot. So when I say it's "just sex" how could it ever be anything more than that? How could it be meaningful after what she did to me? After what she said to me that Saturday morning

before her wedding? I'm not an idiot, Katie. I know what this means to her. And it has always meant even less to me.

3:58pm:

But Jake, you don't do that when you love someone else. Not because it's "just sex," but because you know it will hurt the person you love if she ever finds out about it.

Jake

3:59pm:

You're right.

4:27pm:

And I'm sorry.

4:47pm:

But please understand my position. I never knew how you felt. I knew you liked it when I said nice things to you, but that's it. Nothing about loving me. And this thing with Rachel really was "just sex." Which is what I needed. You kept pushing me away all weekend, wouldn't even let me put my hand on your leg at dinner. Or cuddle into you at the beach fire. Or kiss you goodnight when we were both way too drunk to be sleeping in the same room. Do you see why I would do what I did? I'm no different than anyone else: I need to feel loved. And not just by anyone. I need to feel loved by you.

6:36pm:

Please tell me when I can see you again. I'll prove my love to you for the rest of my life if I have to. I'll wait for you to love me. Forever if I have to.

Saturday June 29, 2013

Jake

9:43am:

Hey.

9:50am:

OK, you're still ignoring me. I'm so sorry about all of this. I really am. I hope you believe me when I tell you that I am seriously having a hard time breathing without you in my life. This week has been easier than it should have been, but I think it's because we texted back and forth on Monday. I love you. I still love you. I always will.

10:33am:

I realize you're reading but not responding. That's okay. And I'll leave you alone, I promise I will. But I thought I'd tell you this final thing before going away. I thought you should know that I have been forever changed by you, Katie. You made and make me a better person. I don't know if it's because of what you're studying to become or if it is that loving you has given me hope that someday I might just have another chance at being with you. Whatever it is, I'm happy. Noticeably happy. And I'm friendly to everyone. Even strangers.

10:35am:
I have you to thank for the improved Jake. I love myself a lot more because you. Thank you.

11:48am:
Hey.

Jake

11:48am:
Katie! I'm so happy you finally responded. How are you?

11:49am:
Today is the first day of the rest of my life, Jake. I thought I should share that with you.

Jake

11:50am:

That sounds a little scary, to be honest with you.

But I hope this new life includes me playing a part in it.

\---

11:50am:

Well, if we're being honest with each other now, I will admit that it IS scary.

\---

Jake

11:50am:

Is this where you break my heart and say you're getting married today?

\---

11:51am:

LOL, not quite. Not even close.

\---

Jake

11:51am:

Then what role do I play?

\---

11:52am:

Let me explain something first. You have changed me too, Jake.

\---

Jake

11:52am:

OK, that's good. Can I see you now? For coffee? Something innocent and happy and with no strings attached.

11:53am:

I'm afraid I actually meant what I said before. About never seeing or hearing from me again. Because you changed me, but not in a positive way. You've ruined me, Jake. I don't think I will ever love someone as much and as wholly as I loved you. So yes, you changed me. But in a bad way, in the worst way possible.

Jake

11:55am:

I'm so sorry, Katie. It breaks my heart that you will remember me that way. Can I see you? I'll come to you, wherever you want to meet. I want to get this little hiccup behind us so we can both move on.

11:56am:

Actually, I'm waiting for someone right now, and then I'm getting on a plane and moving back home. I'm taking some time away from school because I'm, well, a little ruined right now and I need to clear my head.

Jake

> 11:57am:
>
> What, really? I'm sorry. I really am. Please let me
> help. I promise I won't hurt you. I promise to be a
> great friend, first and foremost. I won't cross the
> line. I just need you in my life. I need to make
> things right with you.

11:59am:

I'm afraid that won't happen, Jake.

Jake

> 11:59am:
>
> Who are you meeting before you leave? Why
> can't I see you one last time?

12:00pm:

OK, you won't like this, but I'm meeting with Rachel's husband. His
name is Will.

Jake

> 12:00pm:

I don't know what to think of that. Are you going to tell him everything?

12:01pm:

Tell him? No. Even though he's a complete stranger, I can't break his heart by telling him that his wife has been fucking you since the before the day she married him. I can't do that to someone. I'm not you.

Jake

> 12:01pm:
>
> Then why are you meeting him? I haven't seen Rachel in about a month. I meant it when I said we were through. Why fuck things up for her when it's me you're angry with?

12:02pm:

I'm not telling him anything. He can draw his own conclusion.

Jake

> 12:02pm:
>
> OK, I'm completely lost now.

12:02pm:

I have two phones, Jake. This one. And another one, which you don't know about. That's the one I'll keep until I see Rachel, and then it's hers. But the one you and I have been texting back and forth on? That's the one I'm giving Will.

Jake

> 12:03pm:
>
> So he can read about my relationship with YOU? I don't see how he'll care about us. Even you don't care and you're part of it.

12:03pm:

Well, mostly so he can read about your relationship with his wife. You've admitted a lot, Jake. I also have a pic of Rachel leaving your apartment. This man is a good person. He's innocent. He deserves to know.

Jake

> 12:06pm:
>
> Where are you? Can we talk about this before you go and fuck up someone else's life?

12:06pm:

You'll never see or hear from me again, Jake. Now I have to go. Will is here.

Jake

> 12:07pm:
>
> You realize you're a selfish fucking cunt, don't you? This has nothing to do with Rachel. It has everything to do with me and you and a woman named Christine that I will never see again.
>
> 12:13pm:
>
> Bitch! I pray (and you should do the same) that I never see your fucking face again!

7:45pm:

Hi.

7:53pm:

Jake, my name is Will. You know who I am, right? And now I know everything. If you try to contact my wife again, I will kill you. Do you understand me?

7:56pm:

I need an answer, Jake. Because if you don't text me back, I will show up at your apartment. You have until 830 to acknowledge my text. At 831, I'm getting my shoes on and taking a walk.

8:11pm:

Tick tock.

Jake

        8:29pm:

        Acknowledged.

8:29pm:

Smart move, Jake.

Jake

        8:31pm:

        Fuck. You.

As the taxi stops outside the building, it finally makes perfect sense where the Samsung came from – Will. He knew as soon as I lost the baby that it wasn't mine. He knew all about Jake. It must have killed him.

"Hey, Lady? You okay?" the driver asks me.

I wipe my eyes. I hate Katie for ruining my life with Will. She broke his heart, she broke Jake's and she tried to break mine. With one phone, that little bitch is responsible for way too much heartache.

"Time to pay," the driver says as if he can read my mind.

"Can you wait? I'll be fifteen minutes."

He sighs. "I wait five. You not here, I leave."

I nod, hurrying out of the car and through the rain to the building. The doorman greets me, then waves me over.

"I'm in a hurry," I tell him. "The cab is waiting."

He steps closer to me, keeps his voice low. "Maria sent a suitcase down for you."

He motions toward his desk; one of the larger Samsonites from our honeymoon waits for me. I won't even get to see the inside of the Penthouse one last time, say goodbye to Maria who shared so many of my secrets. Then again, it seems her loyalties lie with Will anyway.

"Can I get the bag for you, Rachel?" he asks.

Grabbing it by the handle, I shake my head, no. I roll it out to the taxi, but the driver gets out to load it into the trunk. It's the first hint he gives me that he has a heart. I get into the car and wait for him, wondering where I should go. Michelle and Romina would likely make room for me. But neither of them are hurting like I am right now. I need someone else. I need-

And then it hits me. I grab the Samsung and take a stab at the dark as the driver gets into the car and asks me where we're going.

"Give a minute."

I tap a quick message in jAppe:

12:48pm:

Jake, are you there? It's Rachel. We need to talk.

"Lady, I'm busy. I need an address."

I rhyme off Jake's address like it's my own.

Except Jake doesn't respond, and that gets me thinking that maybe he meant it when he told me it was over that last time he bent me over his bed and filled me with his honey from behind. I love it when he comes inside me, love the warmth of having him with me for the rest of the day.

I tap away again.

12:53pm:

Text me when you can. Will knows everything. I'm using the key you gave me two months ago. I need a place to crash. And we need to talk about what you said about me to Katie. Asshole.

And we *would* talk. Well, most likely I would yell and he would try to make shit up. And while it hurts to know that he said those things, I know that Jake loves me. Still. Always.

At last, the Samsung vibrates in my hand.

It's a message. From Jake.

Jake

> 12:55pm:
>
> I'm coming home. Be there in half an hour. Make
> yourself at home.

12:55pm:

Thank you.

Jake

> 12:56pm:
>
> Should I bring anything home with me?

12:57pm:

Just your "appetite."

Jake

> 12:58pm:

Don't worry about that. I'm always hungry for you.

12:59pm:

And after, we'll talk about Katie.

Jake

      12:59pm:

      I'm sorry if you read everything. I guess I'll have to

      make sure I last extra long, then.

Tapping away at the keys, I'm smiling at his sense of humor, even

though I will rip him a new one after he's done fucking me.

1:00pm:

Jake, I'm pissed about what you said.

Jake

      1:00pm:

      But you still love me. Right...?

1:01pm:

Of course I do. And you still love me. Right...?

Jake

      1:01pm:

      I never stopped. I never will. Just like I promised.

1:02pm:

You promised Katie the same thing.

Jake

      1:02pm:

      Touché. I'll see you in a bit.

I'm still smiling as we arrive at Jake's building. The driver gets out of the car and helps me with getting the suitcase out of the trunk. I give him a decent tip and I'm walking toward the front door when I hear him call at me.

"Lady. You forgot this."

I turn around and he's waving a phone at me. I give him a smile, then shake my head. "It's not mine. Toss it in the lost and found bin or something. I don't want it."

He frowns like I'm crazy. I take that as my cue to walk away. So that's why I do.

Jake will be home soon and I want to have a shower, get under the sheets so there's no wasting time. We have a lot of time to make up for.

A Sneak Peek Into:

Christine's Return

A Textual Encounters Story

Suicide can be a tough pill to swallow if you don't like taking pills in the first place. But in all fairness, ever since I pissed blue on the home pregnancy test a little more than three months ago, even swallowing a limp noodle triggers my gag reflex – and here I'm talking about a larger noodle, like Fusilli or, oh god, I'm gagging just thinking about it, Rigatoni. So trying to swallow a couple of expired OxyContins at Jake's bathroom sink simply doesn't want to work.

Because just when I think I've got one down, it comes projecting its way back up, forcing me to my knees in front of the toilet. It might sound shallow of me, but I don't want him to find me in a pile of my own vomit. It's not only unlady-like, but my plan will backfire.

So yeah, staging this suicide is a tough

pill to swallow, which is exactly what I'm thinking about when I hear the noise outside the bathroom.

He's home.

I creep up to the closed bathroom door and listen. And that's when I hear the woman's voice. My first thought: WTF?

She says to him: "I'll be right back." Which is woman-code for she needs to go to the bathroom. And I'm in it. Shit.

I step away from the door and study the small floor. Shit.

I hadn't planned on him bringing this young whore home. She's too young for him and although I realize he has been making love to her since I eased out of the picture, I also know that they've had a tough time getting along. Again, she's young which means *high maintenance*.

Acting quickly, I take a spot on the floor, turn my head to the side, and freeze in a runner's pose that I'm sure looks like something out of a CSI episode. That's when I realize the pills are still in my hand. Shit.

Outside, I hear the footsteps.

I let a dozen pills slip out of the

canister, then close my eyes as the bathroom door opens and catches on my foot.

The young girl stifles a scream.

And Jake asks: "Everything okay?"

The girl doesn't say anything. Because she's in work mode, kneeling beside me, taking my pulse. I open my eyes a crack and see her counting seconds off her watch. She doesn't look as young up close and her hair seems a little darker than I thought. I snap my eyes back shut when her attention shifts and she touches my swelling belly.

"Pregnant," she whispers. "But alive. Good vitals."

She pulls the pills out of my hand and studies the canister.

"This isn't…" she whispers. "Oh, I know you." She gives me a shake, as if to wake me up, then leans in close. I feel something sliding into my pocket. "I know you're not dead. I'm not a fucking idiot."

I reach down and seize her wrist, stopping her. I recognize the feel of my iPhone in an instant.

"Well, well," she says. "Nice to finally meet you." She pats my belly. "I'm guessing you're not bloated."

"Who. Are. You?"

"I'm the girl Jake's in love with."

"It's time for you to get back to your babysitter… Katie." I pat my belly this time. "Your fuck buddy is going to be a daddy, and I need to have an adult conversation with him."

Katie looks confused but then she stands, smirks at me and crosses her arms. I can see in the mirror's reflection that she has a tattoo on the back her neck. It surprises me that Jake likes this girl.

"Jake!" I call out.

"You really want to do this?" Katie asks.

"How'd you get my iPhone?" I ask, pulling it from my pocket.

"The Tooth Fairy. You'd think someone as careful as you would have known how to lock the screen."

"Blame it on the pregnancy-" I start, but stop when-

Jake appears at the door.

His eyes go wide at the sight of me. "Christine," he says in a sucker-punched kind of way. "What are you doing here?"

I rub my belly while staring him down.

"Who is this?"

Jake doesn't even look at her and I can sense the stinging in her eyes. It sucks being someone's second choice. I remember feeling that way about Rachel.

"Jake," I say with a quiver in my voice. "It's been horrible."

"Where have you been?" he asks me.

"Hiding. From Peter. He'll kill me if he sees me like this." I stare down at my belly, give it another rub so as to hammer the point home.

"Holy shit," he says. "Is that…?"

I give a nod in Katie's direction. "Jake, can we speak in private? Maybe send the girl guide home?"

"Sure. Yes. Yes, I'm sorry." He faces Katie at last, and she simply shakes her head. The redness on her cheeks is a telling tale of her burnt disappointment.

"Fuck you, Jake. When this whore breaks your heart again, don't call me." She turns to leave, but comes back and fires a fist at Jake's nose. "Asshole."

At last, she leaves, slamming doors and knocking stuff to the floor as she goes.

Funny, even though I expected her to look younger, a lot younger, she behaves exactly like a teenager would. Oh well, not everyone ages well and Katie was a perfect example of that.

I let out a chuckle, and then Jake chuckles behind the hand holding his nose. When he pulls his hand away from his face, there's a little bit blood just like there would have been in a movie. But not like when Peter used to beat me to a pulp, not bloody like that.

I open my arms to him, and he melts into me, squeezing me tight. Then he notices the pills on the floor.

"What's going on?" he asks.

"I wanted…"

"You wanted *what*?"

"I wanted to get your attention."

He rubs my belly. "You've got my attention with *this*." He takes my hand and leads me out of the bathroom to the sofa where we made love seventy-seven days ago. I've missed him. A lot.

"This isn't a happy story, Jake," I tell him.

He frowns, uncertain. "Is this… am I the…?"

"Yes, of course! You're the father. But getting here wasn't easy. Peter is a lunatic. He will kill you. And me. You realize that, right?"

The frown deepens. "What are you talking about?"

"Have you heard about Eduardo Moreno? In the building across the street?"

The color drains for his face and he nods. Everyone in Manhattan has heard about Eduardo being found in a dumpster after someone beat him to death. Incredibly, the police still haven't tracked Peter down and arrested him for the murder.

"He died for us, Jake. He died so I could get here. To be with you."

That scares him a little more, and I feel him withdraw a tad. Understandable. Someone died for his happiness, but that's just how things work in real life. Look at the brave soldiers who fight our wars. The way I see it, Eduardo was a soldier too. He made a sacrifice for the greater good of my love for Jake.

"He died for us?" he asks. I don't blame

him for coming across as a little retarded – he *has* been spending a lot of time with Katie after all.

"Do you want to hear the story? Or just get caught up in the minutia?"

He takes a big gulp of air. "Okay, let's hear it."